Yellow Star

by Jennifer Roy

MARSHALL CAVENDISH

To my mother, Robin Rozines

Text copyright © 2006 by Jennifer Roy
Jacket photo © 2006 by George C. Beresford/Getty Images

Marshall Cavendish Corporation
99 White Plains Road
Tarrytown, NY 10591
www.marshallcavendish.us

Library of Congress Cataloging-in-Publication Data
Roy, Jennifer Rozines, 1967-
Yellow star / by Jennifer Roy.
p. cm.
Summary: From 1939, when Syvia is four and a half years old, to 1945 when she has just turned ten, a Jewish girl and her family struggle to survive in Poland's Lodz ghetto during the Nazi occupation.
ISBN-13: 978-0-7614-5277-5
ISBN-10: 0-7614-5277-X
1. Jews—Persecutions—Poland—Lódz—Juvenile fiction. 2. Holocaust, Jewish (1939-1945)—Poland—Juvenile fiction. [1. Jews—Poland—Fiction. 2. Holocaust, Jewish (1939-1945)—Poland—Fiction. 3. Family life—Poland—Fiction. 4. Poland—History—Occupation, 1939-1945—Fiction.] I. Title.
PZ7.R812185Yel 2006
[Fic]—dc22
2005050788

The text of this book is set in 12-point Aldine.
Book design by Alex Ferrari

Printed in The United States of America
First edition
10 9 8 7 6 5 4 3 2

mc Marshall Cavendish

Acknowledgments

Special thanks to my twin sister, Julia DeVillers (an amazing author), and my sister Amy Rozines. Also, thank you to my editor, Margery Cuyler, and to Michelle Bisson.

This book would not have existed if it weren't for Sylvia Perlmutter Rozines and her courageous testimony. This work also honors the memory of Samuel Rozines, David Rozines, Rachel Rozines, and Isaac and Dora Perlmutter.

Many thanks to Gregory Rozines, Harriet Diller, Gwen Rudnick, Gail Aldous, Karen Hesse, Jane Yolen, Sharon Aibel, and Quinn and Jack DeVillers.

Finally, I am profoundly grateful to my husband, Gregory, and son, Adam, for bringing me so much joy.

Prologue

"In 1939, the Germans invaded the town of Lodz, Poland. They forced all of the Jewish people to live in a small part of the city called a ghetto. They built a barbed-wire fence around it and posted Nazi guards to keep everyone inside it. Two hundred and seventy thousand people lived in the Lodz ghetto.

"In 1945, the war ended. The Germans surrendered, and the ghetto was liberated. Out of more than a quarter of a million people, only about 800 walked out of the ghetto. Of those who survived, only twelve were children.

"I was one of the twelve."

—*Excerpt from interview with Sylvia Perlmutter,*
March 2003

Introduction

This is the true story of Syvia, now called Sylvia, Perlmutter. When World War II began, she was four and a half years old. When it ended, she was ten.

For more than fifty years after the war, Syvia, like many Holocaust survivors, did not talk about her experiences.

But as she grew older, it was time. Time to remember. Time to share. Memories were coming back to her in dreams. Details popped into her head during the day. Syvia's story was bursting to the surface, demanding to be told.

So she told it to me, her niece.

For the first time, I heard a survivor's story from start to finish.

When I learned that my aunt, now called Sylvia, was one of the twelve children who survived the Lodz ghetto, I was stunned. *How come we didn't know this about her?*

I asked my aunt to tell me a little about it. And I

asked if it would be all right if I tape-recorded her. She agreed. So over the telephone, long-distance from her apartment in Maryland to my house in upstate New York, Sylvia talked. The more she spoke, the more she remembered. That got me thinking.

I was a published author, and I wondered if I could narrate her story. But was I the right person to write it? I have always been afraid of *anything* relating to the Holocaust. As a Jewish child I grew up aware of it, because every year in Hebrew school I saw films of Holocaust atrocities. Piles of dead children's shoes, mass graves of bones, skeletal survivors being liberated. But the teachers never explained these in a historical context so that we could understand it. No Holocaust curriculum or discussions back then. Just images of one of the worst periods in modern history. The murder of 6 million Jews.

As an American Jewish girl, I grew up knowing that the world was not always a safe place, that people could turn on you, even in a civilized society. The Holocaust was something huge and unimaginable. Terrifying and traumatic. But it was also something nobody talked about. Ask a Holocaust survivor a question about it, and he or she is likely to change the subject. When I was growing up in the suburbs of upstate New York, my family talked about everything *but* the war. The survivors' motto was "Never forget!" But the survivors I knew didn't tell me what to remember. Even my dad.

My father, Sam, lived through the Holocaust. Along with his mother, sister, and three brothers, he narrowly escaped being sent to a concentration camp in Poland. My grandfather, my father's father, was separated from his family and killed in the Black Forest massacres in Germany. The remaining members of the family fled to a refugee camp in Siberia. My dad spent his childhood in that camp, struggling to survive until the war ended. My father rarely discussed it. When he died, his story was lost.

Aunt Sylvia was my father's brother's wife. It seemed an honor to listen to her, to be trusted as the guardian of her memories. I vowed to do her story justice.

And then . . . I ran into trouble. First I tried to write the story as a straight nonfiction account. Too dry. Next, I rewrote it in the third person narrative. But that didn't quite work, either. Frustrated, I went back to the tapes and listened again to my aunt's lilting, European-accented voice. Suddenly, the voices of all my Jewish relatives came flooding back to me. American English tinged with Yiddish and Polish, with anxiety and resilience. The voices of my grandma, my uncles, my dad. All now deceased. And that's when I knew that I would write my aunt's story in the first person, as if she were telling the story herself.

This book is written for all my relatives—for my grandmother, Rachel, who left Siberia after the war. She split up her children—sending the oldest to the new Jewish homeland, Israel. She took the other three to America, settling in upstate New York. The baby of their family was Sam, my father. The next youngest was Nathan. Then came David, who fell in love with and married Sylvia Perlmutter. My aunt Sylvia, known when she was younger as Syvia. One of the twelve surviving children of the Lodz ghetto. When my aunt recounted her childhood to me, she spoke as if looking through a child's eyes. She made her experiences feel real, immediate, *urgent*. In the poetry of a survivor's words, this is Syvia's story.

Part One

Before the Second World War, 233,000 Jews lived in the city of Lodz, Poland. They made up one-third of the city's total population and were the second largest Jewish community in Poland.

Many of the Jewish people in Lodz were educated professionals. They were businesspeople, schoolteachers, scientists, and artists. Parents raised their children to be productive citizens.

Meanwhile, in Germany, Adolf Hitler had risen to power. Hitler believed that certain people he called Aryans were superior to others of "inferior" races. Although Judaism is a religion, not a race, Hitler claimed that Jewishness was in a person's blood. His plan to create a "master race" did not include Jews.

On September 1, 1939, the German Nazis invaded Poland, starting the Second World War. The Nazis prepared to isolate Poland's Jews in designated areas called ghettos. One of the ghettos was Lodz. It had 31,721 apartments—most with just one room and no running water. In the spring, 160,000 Jewish men, women, and children walked into the Lodz ghetto. On May 1, 1940, the ghetto was sealed off by a barbed-wire fence. The Jews were isolated from the rest of Poland and cut off from the outside world.

 **FALL 1939**

How It Begins

I am four and a half years old, going on five,
hiding in my special place behind the armchair in
the parlor,
brushing my doll's hair,
listening.
The worry of grown-ups fills the air,
mingling with the lemony smell of the just-baked
cake cooling on the serving platter.
Clink, clink, Mother's teacup trembles on its saucer.
"Must we go, Isaac?" she says to my father, who has
come home from work
unexpectedly,
interrupting the weekly tea.
"We must leave Lodz right away," Papa says. "This
city is unsafe for Jews."
Stroke, stroke, my hand keeps brushing
my doll's hair.
My mind freezes
on one word—
Jews.
Jews.

We are Jews.

I am Jewish.
We observe the Jewish holidays
and keep kosher,
but that is all I know.
What does it matter that we are Jews?
I whisper the question into my doll's ear.
She just stares back at me.

Questions
I do not ask Mother or Papa until later,
after the aunts leave,
the lemon cake untouched.
I am too shy to speak in front of visitors,
even the aunts
who pinch my cheeks
and give me hair bows for my braids.
My aunts are Jewish, my uncles and cousins, too.
Is my doll Jewish?

No one responds to my questions.
They are too busy putting things into suitcases—
forks, knives, cups,

the photo of my parents on their wedding day,
items of clothing,
some for me and some for my older sister, Dora.

"Hush, Syvia," Mother tells me
when I ask more questions,
so I go back to my hiding place
behind the armchair . . .
and wait.

The Journey
It is midnight, but
no one in my family
is sleeping.
We are joggling up and down,
side to side,
traveling to Warsaw
under cover of darkness and forest
in the back of a buggy
pulled by a horse.
Even huddled near me, Mother,
Dora, Aunt Sara, and my two little cousins
cannot keep me warm.
My fingers are icy sticks.

I'm afraid they will snap
like the twigs that are
crackling into pieces under the wagon wheels.

When I say *War-Saw*,
two clouds of cold air puff from my mouth.

My father and Uncle Shmuel sit up front
and take turns driving.
The trip is long.

When we arrive in Warsaw,
for a couple of days
we search for a place to live.

No one will rent to us.
Sorry, no jobs.
It is wartime.
We are Jews.

We return to our home in Lodz.
The trip back
seems even colder.

The Star of David

Orange
is the color of my coat
with matching muffler
that I got as a present
before the war.
Dora got the same set,
only larger and in blue.

Yellow
is the color of
the felt six-pointed star
that is sewn onto my coat.
It is the law
that all Jews have to wear the
Star of David
when they leave their house,
or else be arrested.

I wish I could
rip the star off
(carefully, stitch by stitch, so as not to ruin
my lovely coat),
because yellow is meant to be

a happy color,
not the color of
hate.

Ghetto
The Nazis closed down
a small section of the city.
They said it is swarming
with infectious disease,
but still,
they ordered all Jews of Lodz
to leave their homes
immediately
and move into that space.
It is called a ghetto.

All the Jews?
That must be more than one hundred!
(One hundred is the largest number I know.)
Papa corrects me.
"Over one hundred thousand people,
maybe twice that."

The Rest of Poland

There are many more people
in Poland
who are not Jews.
They are staying in their homes.
That doesn't seem fair.

Dora says they were our neighbors,
but they aren't our friends anymore.
Many of the Polish people have been
saying mean things and
beating and tormenting Jews.

"They hate us," says Dora.
"They are happy we are leaving."

 **FEBRUARY 1940**

Relocation
I am walking
into the ghetto.
My sister holds my hand
so that I don't
get lost
or trampled
by the crowd of people
wearing yellow stars,
carrying possessions,
moving
into the ghetto.

New Home
The first time
we enter the small apartment
on the second floor,
we look around the two rooms.
Mother raises an eyebrow and frowns.
Papa shrugs.
"*Nu*," he says,
"what can we do but make the best of it?"

My sister says,
"Our real home is much nicer."
I want to know where the toilet is.
"Outside the apartment building,
in the courtyard," says Papa.
We will have to share it with all the other families.

The Toilet
The bathroom is tiny.
There are no windows.
I'm careful to lock the door
behind me.

I peel off my mittens,
my coat,
my layers—
I have to go so badly!
I sit on the toilet just in time.

It is so dark in here.
I feel so alone.
What if I can't get out?
What if I'm trapped in this toilet, and nobody hears me?
At home they would hear me and rescue me,

but here it is different.
Why does everything have to be
different now? Why won't they let us go home?
I finish up and push open the door,
holding my breath.
It opens.
I exhale with relief and walk back
into the building,
through the hallway,
to our new life.

Relatives
Papa's and Mother's parents, my grandparents,
are dead,
but I have many aunts and uncles.
Mother's sisters—Sara and Rose and Malka.
Her brothers—Label and Herschel.
They are all living in the ghetto now
with my cousins.
Papa's brother Haskel and his half sisters—
Edit and Esther and Sura—
are in the ghetto, too, with their children.
Papa's brother Luzer lives in Russia
and his half brother, Joseph, lives in Paris, France.

I have many cousins, too.
Everybody is very busy now
or far away
so I don't see my relatives much.
But it is good to belong to a large family,
even when we can't be together.

The Flour Man
In the ghetto
Papa has a job
delivering flour
to stores and bakeries.
Of course, now,
most of the baked goods
go to the Germans,
since our rations
allow only brown bread.
Before the war, Papa worked as a salesman.
He worked hard
and made a good living.
We were not rich.
"Comfortable," Mother called our family.
My parents dressed up
and went out to the theater and to movies.

Now when Papa arrives home from work,
he and Mother don't go anywhere.
Papa is very, very tired.
I sit on his lap and comb his hair.
I kiss his flour-dusted face
and taste his sweetness,
imagining cookies and pastries.
Then Mother gives Papa a
cloth so he can wash up
for dinner.
Plain round bread again.

Women's Work
Mother and Dora
work in a factory
that makes ladies' underwear.
Dora says Polish women outside the ghetto
must eat very well,
because some of the underwear
is very, very large.

Dora had to lie
about her age
to get work.

She said she was fourteen,
although she's really only twelve.
The Germans place greater value
on Jews who work,
my father told her.
So during the day,
when our parents work,
Dora watches me.
Then in the evenings,
she goes to work.

"Am I not valuable to the Germans?"
I ask Papa.
"You are valuable to this family," he says,
"and that is enough."

 **SUMMER 1940**

The Fence

A fence has been built
around
us.
The ghetto is now a cage
with iron wires.
We are
sealed in.

Mother says,
"Good. Now we are protected
from the Poles."

Father says, "No,
now we are at the mercy
of the Nazis.
They are holding us here until they decide
how they will
get rid of us."

Hava and Itka

I have some new friends—

Hava and Itka.
We play dress up
with our dolls,
and sometimes
we play house.
A neighbor made us
three rag dolls
from stuffed sheets.
She drew the faces on with pencil.
We are learning
to sew
clothes for our dolls
from scraps of fabric.
Hava sews the best,
and Itka is the smartest.
Hava's little brother
is dying of cancer,
so we often give Hava the
best scraps
to cheer her up.

Food

I am standing with my mother
in the long, long line that is

snaking up to the door
of the grocery.
We are waiting to buy
our ration of black bread.
Each person gets a certain amount.
Never enough, it seems.

I am thinking of the
coming summer,
when the vegetables
we planted in the tiny plot of land
in the backyard garden
will be ready to pick.

Then we can have soup
with our bread.
That will make Mother happy.
She tries to make up
new recipes
with such little food
(but with lots of salt,
for some reason there is always salt).
At the grocery,
there are vegetables.

Sometimes we can buy a small piece of meat,
which I later find out comes from horses.

On a really good day
the men Papa works with
gather together
and shake the flour dust
that has collected in their pockets,
flour spilled from openings
in the seams
of the fabric delivery bags.
They place the dust on a scale
and combine the flour,
then divide it equally
among the men.
("It is important to be honest," Papa says.)
Sometimes there is enough flour
for mother to make noodles.
I hope today is one of those days,
because before we have
even reached the front of the grocery line,
the grocer stands at the door and shouts,
"No more bread!
All out!"

Colors of the Ghetto

Papa and I are walking hand in hand to a place
where he does business.
The streets are so crowded,
it's a wonder that we have enough
air to breathe.
As Papa pulls me along, I see
brown shoes, brown pants legs, brown dresses,
brown road.
I look up at the brown buildings
and the cloud of brown dust and smoke
that hangs in the sky.
Bright colors
don't exist in the ghetto,
except for the yellow stars
and puddles of red blood
that we carefully step around.
"More shootings," Papa says quietly.
His face is gray.

The Guard

Uniform. Boots. Gun. Cigarette.
The German guard
stands at the fence.

Dora and I must pass by him
on our walk to Aunt Sara's apartment.
Dora looks straight ahead.
I look down at my feet.
Step, step.
Thump, thump, my heart is racing,
but my feet walk
as if they have nothing to fear.

I do not think of the things
I have been hearing,
like the story of a boy
who went out for bread
and was shot by a guard
who didn't like the way the boy
looked at him.

Like the woman
who went crazy
and ran straight into the fence
and was shot.

Like the man who was
dragged off and shot

in front of his two children.
No one knows why.

All these stories took place
along the fence.
But there are many other stories
happening inside this fence, inside this ghetto,
that I cannot think about
right now,
because the guard is lifting up his arm
(*To shoot his gun?*)
to light his cigarette,
and I must keep walking.

 **FALL 1940**

No School

Dora is particularly grouchy today.
She sits on her bed,
pick-pick-picking
at her fingernails.

When I say, "What's wrong?"
she gives me a sour face,
so I back away,
but then she tells me that today
would have been the first day of school.

I remember
the first day of school last year.
Dora dressed up in a new outfit,
twirling in the kitchen with excitement
over entering the junior high.
Dora had a lot of friends,
girls and boys,
and teachers liked her, too.

"Now I'm here," Dora says,

"working in a factory,
watching my baby sister.
I wonder if anyone from my old school
even notices that I am gone?"
My sister looks down at her hands.
Pick. Pick.

Kindergarten
Today
would have been my first day
of kindergarten.
I imagine shiny classroom floors,
sunny windows, a clean chalkboard,
and a smiley teacher
who says, "Welcome, Syvia!"

I ask Dora
to teach me the alphabet.
She takes a stick
and draws letters in the dirt.
Dora is not very smiley,
but she does say good
when I get things right.
It starts to rain. It is time to go inside,

but I slip in the dirt,
landing on my bottom.
"Uh-oh," I say,
"I've wiped out *A*."
I'm worried that Dora will yell at me
for getting muddy, but instead
she sits down, too, mud and all.

"What letter am I covering?" she asks.
"*D*," I say (just guessing).
"Good," my sister replies.
Then we both laugh,
feeling the earth squish beneath us.

Motorcycles

Vrrrroooommmmm . . . sputsputspop . . . vrroomm!
Motorcycles race around the streets.
Nazi soldiers drive by our building,
trailing clouds of black smoke.
"They drive like crazies," Mother complains.
Papa laughs and says,
"Why should people with no regard
for human life
follow the rules of traffic?"

Playing Games

Itka, Hava, and I
are standing by the windowsill
looking down
at a small group of boys
playing a game with stones.
Up. Down. Up. Down.
I don't know the rules,
but it's something to do with
tossing the stones in the air
and catching them.

"See that boy?" Itka points.
"The one with the black cap?
He is a smuggler."
He sneaks
through a hole in the fence
and sells things
to the Polish people,
then brings things back
to the Jewish people.

"If he gets caught," Itka says,
"the Germans will kill him."

"They might torture him first,"
Hava adds.

I watch the boy play with the stones for a moment.
"Let's play dolls," I say.
So we do.

Making Clothes
Sometimes I help
the women in our building
make clothes.
They give me an old sweater
that has holes,
and I pull apart the yarn.
The women use the yarn
along with pieces of old fabric
to make dresses and sweaters.
They must find ways to be warm,
they say,
since winter is coming soon.
There will be no heat
in the building.
I feel the wool
thread through my fingers,

soft and thick and ready
to help.

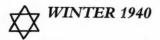 **WINTER 1940**

Mourning

Hava's brother died,
so we visit her family.
They are sitting shiva,
the Jewish mourning time,
in their dark apartment, lit only by a candle.

Hava looks very solemn.
Her mother is weeping.
"We are sorry for your loss," Papa says.
I feel like I am suffocating in my too-small dress
and itchy woolen tights.
I have brought my doll, although
I see now it was a mistake.
Of course we will not play.
Not now.

I had to carry my doll in my arms
over to Hava's,
because I no longer have a carriage.
Father chopped it up
to use for firewood.

People are dying in this ghetto,
not just Hava's brother.
Nobody has died who is close to me—
my aunts, uncles, and cousins are okay,
as are my parents and sister.

But around us people are dying,
some even in my building.
There are many dark apartments in Lodz,
boxes of grief and fear.

When we are back home,
I close my eyes tightly,
and in my mind I see a giant bubble
floating down from the sky,
circling our apartment,
my family.
For a few moments,
I feel a little bit safe.

Rumkowski

On payday,
Papa brings home a little money.
Mother and Dora bring a little, too.
They place the bills in a small pile

on the table.
I pick up one bill.
It feels crisp and new.
It is "ghetto money"
with a man's face printed on it.
Who is this man with the fluffy white hair?

"He is Rumkowski," Papa tells me.
Rumkowski is the *Judenalteste*,
elder of the Jews.
The Nazis put him in charge
of running the ghetto.
He watches over the factories and the banks
and the post office and all of the food.
No one knows why this one man
was chosen to speak for all the Jews.
What we do know is that the more
"Rumkies" pile up on our table,
the more we will eat this week.

Rations
Ration cards
tell how much food and supplies
each person in the ghetto is allowed.
For working, Papa, Mother, and Dora

get one bowl of thin barley-bean soup,
a slice from a loaf of bread,
a little vegetable (often beets),
and brown water called coffee
every day.
I get scraps they have saved
and pieces of food the neighbors give me.
A growing girl needs food, they say,
as they slip me bits of things
that do not taste at all
like the food Mother used
to cook at home.

Before.

Sweet pastries, soups thick with meat and noodles,
chewy bread with fruit spread,
even green beans.
I used to not like green beans,
but now I'd eat them all up.

A Big Girl
Dora has been switched to the day shift
at the factory,

so during the afternoons,
when everyone else is at work,
I have to spend time in neighbors' apartments.
I am allowed to leave our place
and walk down certain hallways and knock
on certain doors,
and someone else's grandmother or aunt
will let me in.

"You can do this now that you are a big girl
of six years old," says Mother.
"I am six?"
Yes, I'm told.
Your birthday was last week.
Oh. Well . . .
Now I can show Hava and Itka my new age,
using the fingers of my two hands
or counting the points
on my yellow star.
Six must be a very important number!

Chills

I do not like winter in the ghetto.
There is too much cold and
not enough food
and no one is in a good mood.
Sometimes when Dora is bored or annoyed,
she pokes me with
a wire hanger.
"If you don't do what I tell you," she hisses,
"the Bad Men will get you."

A couple of times she does this after my bedtime,
her shadow looming over me,
her warning chilling my bones.
It is rare to feel warm in the winter.

PART TWO

During 1941, thousands of Jews from other countries were moved into the Lodz ghetto. They came from Germany, Austria, Czechoslovakia, and Luxembourg. Conditions in the already overcrowded ghetto became even worse. Many people died of illness, including typhus fever. Others froze to death. The worst problem, however, was starvation. The average daily food ration per person was about 1,000 calories. The quality of food was very poor. Dirt, ground glass, and other particles were found in the flour, and the only food available was often rotten.

With fuel in short supply, the winter was especially harsh on ghetto residents. The people of Lodz were struggling to stay alive. On December 7, 1941, the United States entered the war after the Japanese attack on Pearl Harbor, Hawaii. Soon after, Germany and Italy declared war on the United States. While the world war raged outside, the "war" inside the Lodz ghetto against the Jews grew worse.

 **SPRING 1941**

Live for Today
Life goes on in the ghetto.
Spring breezes blow through
the wire fence.
The mood becomes brighter with the sun.

Life goes on in the ghetto.
There are weddings and dances and songs.
Mothers take their new babies
outside to show them off to the neighborhood.
Pink faces swaddled in blankets stitched with
yellow stars.

Life goes on in the ghetto.
The grown-ups here have a saying:
"Live for today,
for tomorrow we may fry in the pan!"

Missing
Hava is missing.
She went for a short walk on the street
and never came back.

Gone,
vanished,
disappeared.

Where is she?
What happened?
Did someone take her?
Is she still alive???

Why Hava???

The ghetto holds its secrets tightly
and shrugs its shoulders
when asked questions.

Tea with the Queen
Itka comes over to my apartment,
but we don't say much.
Our dolls do the talking for us.

Itka's doll: Where is our friend today?
My doll: I don't know.
Itka's doll: Perhaps she had another engagement.
My doll: More important than our weekly tea?

Silence.

Itka's doll: I bet she's meeting with the queen!

My doll: Of course! Tea with the queen is a good reason.

Our dolls nod, satisfied.

Itka and I sit on the bare floor
imagining royal velvet-cushioned chairs
and jewel-encrusted teacups
and Hava and her doll nibbling finger sandwiches
between sips.

Of course, deep down we know
that there is no queen
inviting little Jewish girls to tea.

Two Sides

It is bedtime, but no one is getting ready for bed.
My parents are arguing in the kitchen area.
Dora and I listen from the sitting area.
Mother says,
"Syvia is not to go outside
without one of us with her."
She bangs a pot with a spoon for emphasis.

Papa says,
"Impossible. She can't stay inside all those hours
while we work. It's too hot, too lonely."
Mother says,
"But it's too dangerous
any other way."

They go back and forth—yes, no (*bang*),
yes, no (*bang*).
Finally, I go over and tug on Papa's sleeve.
"I don't mind staying inside.
I don't want Mother to worry."
Dora rolls her eyes at me and mouths,
Such a good girl.

The truth is, I don't want to go out
by myself.
But I also don't want Papa to think
I'm not brave.

Dreams
That night I am poked awake
by Dora's fingers.
"Shhh . . . ," she whispers, "come with me."

I climb over Mother, careful not to kick Papa,
and stumble behind Dora over to her bed.

"Come in," Dora says.
We lie down under the thin blanket.
Nighttime seems different over here,
more grown-up.
Dora tells me she had a bad dream
that I went missing, just like Hava.

"We looked and looked but you were
nowhere," she says.
Her voice is snuffly, shaky, un-Doralike.

Just before we both drift back to sleep,
Dora gives me a hug.
"I will protect you, baby sister," she whispers
fiercely.

I don't mind being called *baby*.
I am warm and sleepy and on my way to
sweet dreams.

My Day
(now that I am not allowed outside)
Wake up.
Say good-bye to Mother, Papa, and Dora
as they go off to work.
Get dressed.
Eat breakfast (leftover soup or bread or
weak coffee).
Clean. Make beds, dust, sweep, move things,
put them back,
wash, wipe, scrape, inspect.
Play with my doll.
Eat lunch (leftover soup or vegetables
or weak coffee).
Lie on my bed and look at the shapes made by
ceiling cracks.
Make up stories about them.
Play with my doll.
Visit neighbors.
Family comes home!
Eat dinner (soup or vegetables and weak coffee).
Go to bed.
Sleep.

Goodbye, Dust!

Sometimes I clean and sing little songs.
"Good-bye, dust!
Hello, shine!
Cobweb in the corner—you can't hide from me!"

It is a fine day when Mother brings home
new rags for cleaning!

 **SUMMER 1941**

The Law

Hava is still missing.
She is not the only one.
Every day the neighbors buzz about who is gone,
who is sick, who died,
who has been murdered.
It could be an old person
or a baby or anybody.

The German soldiers (Nazis) who keep us here
do not care if we are sick or starving,
alive or dead.
They beat people and shoot them right
in front of everyone,
and no one can say anything,
because the Nazis are the law.

I do not understand this.
How can a person kill another person?
It hurts my heart.
I don't want my family or friends to die.
I don't want a Nazi to notice me and think,

Jew.
Because then I might die, too.

The Woman in the House
Dora and I are going to visit Aunt Sara.
The sun tickles my pale skin,
then burns.
We have to walk along the fence.
Dora meets a girl she knows from work
and stops to chat.
I can see through the fence to the outside,
where the Polish people live.
The ones who aren't Jewish.

I see a white house with red geraniums in front.
What is it like to have flowers in your garden?
We only have vegetables.
It seems like a dream to live outside the ghetto.
The houses look so bright and clean.

A woman comes out of the white house
with a dog.
I would like to have a dog, but of course
there are no pets in the ghetto.

They would be killed for meat.

There are some places along the fence
where there are sometimes no guards.
A person could slip between the wires,
out of the ghetto.
But even if a soldier didn't shoot you
and you got away,
a Polish person would see you
and call the Nazi police
and they would kill you.

It's sad to think that the woman who lives in the
white house
would do that, but she would,
even if she is nice to her dog.

Another Loss
More bad news.
My doll is gone.
When I ask Papa and Mother where she is,
they say shush.
Papa's eyes are sad, though,
and somehow I know that he had to sell her

(like the other things we have sold)
for money or food.

I try very hard
to not make a fuss.
I am a big girl now,
I tell myself,
I do not need dolls.
Of course it's not true.
There's no best friend like a doll.
Like *my* doll.

I observe mourning for seven days.
After that I make a doll out of a rag
and two buttons.

 **FALL 1941**

Love

Dora came home from work in a bad mood.
Mother and Papa are tired.
I miss my real doll.
And we are all hungry.
But there is not enough food for dinner.
Mother does not eat her meal.
She gives it to me instead.
She does not say "I love you" in hugs or kisses,
but her love fills my plate,
and I gobble it up.

Papa says Mother is a noble woman.
He tells me,
"From pain your mother gave you life,
through pain she continues to give."
I think about Papa's words as I finish my broth.
It hurt Mama to give me life? Why?
Didn't I just pop out of her belly button?
I guess I think these words out loud, because
suddenly everyone is looking at me.
Then they all burst into laughter.

Papa, Dora, even Mother.

"Syvia, you are a tonic
for helping us forget our pain,"
says Papa,
and they all smile at me.
Their love fills the air around me,
and I gulp it down.

Hungry
Food and wood and coal
have been rationed even more,
and everybody says,
How will we survive the winter?

And now we hear that 20,000
more people
are being moved into the ghetto.

I am very hungry all the time now,
and we are all quite thin.
Dora, who is nice to me these days,
tells me what it is like to taste butter, eggs, milk,
chocolate.
She says she hopes to fatten me up with her words.

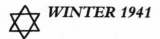 # WINTER 1941

Imagining
Winter
erases whole families.
It has also erased the vegetables
that we grew in our yard,
a whole summer's worth of vegetables.
There weren't enough to last us through the fall.
Now the ground is frozen,
bare.

My family
is weak and starving
but we are still together,
still alive.

Each day seems never ending.
Once, when I am alone in the apartment,
I think I might freeze to death.
Then under the mattress
I find a precious matchstick.
I light a lamp
and lean my face into it,
closing my eyes.

I am on a beach under a hot sun.
Waves of warm blue water slap in and out with the tide.
I sit in the glow of my pretend sun for a
long, long time,
until the lamp burns out and it is once more
winter.

PART THREE

In January 1942, the Nazis began deporting people from the Lodz ghetto. They ordered people onto trains, telling them they were needed to work elsewhere.

This was a lie.

The Nazis had planned their "Final Solution" to the Jewish problem. They built concentration camps, also called extermination camps. The ghettos were like holding cages, keeping Jews penned in until the Nazis decided what to do with them. Extermination camps were the answer. These camps contained gas chambers, where Jews were gassed to death. Their bodies were then piled into crematory ovens and burned to ashes.

Beginning on January 16, 1942, the deportations from the Lodz ghetto went directly to the Chelmno extermination camp. Over the next four months, 55,000 Jews and 5,000 Gypsies were transported to Chelmno.

For a while, the deportations stopped. Then in September, they began again. But it was worse this time. German soldiers entered the ghetto and dragged Jews from their homes, from hospitals, and off the streets. The Germans declared a curfew in the ghetto, the Gehsperre *(ban on movement). Survivors of this brutal time called it the* Sperre.

The Sperre*'s main focus was on children under the age of ten and adults over sixty-five. Chaim Rumkowski, leader of the Jews, announced the news that the children were to be taken away. He said, "I have to cut off limbs to save the body," meaning he had to let the children go in order to save everyone else. Parents were reassured that their children were being taken to a better, safer place.*

Again, it was a lie. They had gone to the Chelmno extermination camp to die.

 **WINTER 1942**

New Worries
Whoooo! Whoooo!
Every day now I hear a train
whistle in the distance.
Deportations have begun.

"What are deportations?" I ask Papa.

"The Nazis are moving people out of the ghetto,"
Papa explains.
"The train takes the people to other places
that need workers."

"Ha!" I hear Dora snort.
She looks up from her mending.
"At the factory they say that the Nazis
are shipping people out
to death camps."

Death camps?

"Shh . . . . shh . . . ." Mother rushes over.
"Not in front of the little one."

Papa gives a stern look to my sister.
"Dora, don't repeat silly talk when you don't know
the whole truth.
They do need more workers elsewhere.
You children should think good thoughts.
Okay, Dora? Syvia?"

"Okay," I say.

"If they need good workers," Dora grumbles,
"why are they crushing hundreds of people
into small cars like cattle?
So their good workers can be
suffocated?"

"Dora!" says Mother.
"Enough!" says Papa.
And then we are all
quiet.

Wedding Invitations
Little papers
are being delivered to many people.

The papers say:
"Be at the train station . . ."
on a certain day
at a certain time.

Everybody in the neighborhood
is calling these papers
"wedding invitations"
and teasing one another.
"Have you been invited to the wedding?"
"Not yet, have you?"

Where exactly are the trains going?
There are rumors,
exaggerations,
stories,
but mostly people just wave the words away
and talk about weddings.

A Happy Night

What a treat!
Itka and her parents are here
for an evening visit.
Itka and I play dress up

with our mothers' shoes and coats.
Even Dora is in a good mood.
She wraps Mother's scarf around her head
and holds our hands as we dance
in a circle.
Around and around.
Until one of my mother's shoes flies off my foot
and hits the wall.
We three take off our shoes and dance some more
in stockinged feet.
Our parents drink weak coffee
and talk in low voices.
Itka and I are comparing our feet
(mine are longer and skinnier).
Then Itka's parents say it's time to leave.

"Thank you for coming," I say in my best
hostess voice.
"Good-bye, Syvia!" Itka smiles and waves
on her way out.
"Bye, see you soon!"

No Friends

Last night with Itka was so happy
but today is the saddest day ever.
Sadness.
Sadness.
Sadness.

Papa took me on his lap and told me this:
On his way home from work,
he passed the train station
and saw Itka's face in one of the windows.
She was looking out
as the train pulled away.

Itka's family had received a summons,
Papa told me.
It had come earlier that week.

I think of Itka
in a train car
packed with people
and Hava
disappearing from the street.
I have no friends anymore,

and I can't even write a letter to Hava or Itka to say,
I miss you,
because I wouldn't know where to
send it.

Silence
One day
there is no train whistle.
After three months of whistles,
deportations have stopped.
My family never received an invitation
to the wedding.
We are still here
in the ghetto!
Is this a good thing?
I guess it is.
We know what to expect here . . .

not very much.

 **SUMMER 1942**

Bean Counting

Summer comes again.
Hot days, sweaty nights.
I am now eight and one-half years old.
One-half is a fraction,
says Dora.
A fraction is part of a whole.

It is summer, so we're gathering a few vegetables
from our brown patch of yard.
Dora breaks a scrawny bean in two.
She pops one piece in her mouth.
"One-half," she explains.
The other goes into my mouth.
Two halves.
I wonder, *if I were in real school,*
would I be smart at arithmetic?

"I'd rather have half of a cream bun," says Dora.
"And if you acted very good,
I'd give you the other half."
Such a nice sister.

That summer we eat a lot of fractions.

Bad News

No.
Oh no.
The Nazis have made a new announcement.
It is too horrible to think about,
so I am hiding under the bedcover
on the big bed
while my parents talk.

"What are we going to do, Isaac?"
"I just don't know."
"We can't let them have her."
"We won't let them have her."
"But, how . . . ?"
"I don't know yet. We will do something."

I am a bear in a cave,
safe from the storms
that rage around me.
I burrow down further into the bed
and fall asleep.

Good-bye, Children!

Give us the children,
the Nazis say.
We will take them to a place
where they will have food and fresh air.
Parents, how lucky you are!
the Nazis say.
You won't have to worry about your children
while you are at work.
They will be cared for by us.

All Jewish children
must report to the train station
for deportation
immediately.
The trains will leave daily at noon,
the Nazis say.

Repeat:
All children
to the train station.
All
Jewish
children.

Coming for the Children

Knock! Knock!
The soldiers are going door-to-door,
thumping their black-gloved fists
until someone lets them in.
Where are the children?
Give us the children!

They come at night,
storming neighborhoods,
kicking in locked doors
with their heavy boots,
searching room to room,
pulling children out from closets,
from under beds,
ripping children from their parents' arms
and dragging them away.

Small children.
Big children.
Crying children.
If parents try to stop the soldiers,
Bang! Bang!
The soldiers shoot them dead.

A Mother's Story
Each night the soldiers
come closer and closer
to our neighborhood.

A few blocks away,
a cousin of my aunt's husband
was home with her two children—
one twelve years old,
the other just four.
The Nazis burst into their house
and said, "Give us the children."
But my aunt's husband's cousin
would not let go.
She held them both tightly in her arms.

One soldier said,
"We don't have time for this foolishness.
Just shoot them all."
The other soldier said,
"No, we need to bring in one more alive tonight,
and, anyway, we are running very low on bullets."

So they said to the woman,

"You are lucky tonight,
you can keep one of the children,
and you will all live."
They made the woman choose.
Then they took one child away.

My aunt told us later
that the woman thought her older son
would have a better chance
of surviving in the ghetto,
so she gave up her little one.
*Maybe they will be kind to such a
small child?*

One Child
This is the story I make up
in my head:

The Nazis come to our building.
We hear their heavy footsteps
thudding down the hallway.
Then they realize it is past dinnertime,
and they are very hungry.
So they go off to their headquarters

for sausages.
And they forget to come back.

Dora says Papa is making a plan,
but she doesn't know what.
My sister has papers that show that she has a job.
The papers say that she is older than she really is,
so the soldiers won't take her.
When they come to our building,
to our apartment,
they will find one child to take.
Me.

They're Here
One night we are finishing our soup
and then . . .
they're here.
The Nazis.
Well, not quite here,
but on the next street over,
close enough for us to hear the shouting
from our open window.

"Syvia," says Papa. "Come here."

I can't move. My legs have stopped working.

"Go with your father," Mother says.
Her voice is firm
but gentle.

I go to Papa.
He puts my coat and hat on me
and says,
"Let's go."

Dora watches with wide eyes.
She is chewing a piece of her hair.
She gives me a weak smile
and waves her fingers.

Then Papa takes my hand
and walks me out the door,
into the dark night.

Escape
Through the hallway,
down the staircase,
out the front door.

Hurry, hurry.
Quiet, quiet.

Across the street
to a tall brick wall
that separates our neighborhood
from an old cemetery.
Up you go,
I'm right behind you.

First Papa lifts me up
and over.
Thud! I land on my hands and knees
on hard dirt.
Papa climbs over
and jumps to the ground.

This way, this way,
Hurry, hurry.

Papa picks me up and takes my hand again,
and we start running.
It is nighttime,
but the moon is shining.

There is just enough light to see
the rows of light-colored gravestones.

Papa pulls me along,
weaving through the stones
until he stops.
So I stop.
We are next to a stone that is a bit
taller and wider
than most others I've seen.

Papa drops to his knees
and pulls something out
from behind the stone.
A shovel.

"Papa, where . . . how?"
I am out of breath from running.
Papa puts his finger up to his mouth
to say shush,
so I am quiet,
and I watch
Papa thrust the shovel
into the soft ground.

The Hole

Dig. Dig. Dig.
Papa works quickly,
scooping and tossing,
until there is a shallow hole
surrounded by mounds of dirt.

Papa stops digging and looks at me.

"Syvia," he whispers, "get in and lie down."
"You will hide here tonight."

Lie down in the hole?
Alone?
I truly mean to obey my papa
and do it because
I always do what Papa says.
I am a good girl.
But I am in a cemetery
in the dark,
and all I can think of are scary things
like dead people and Nazis,
and instead of lying down in the hole,
I scream:

"No! No!"

"No! No!"
I can't stop screaming.

"Syvia!" Papa rushes over to me
and pulls me into his arms.
My face is pushed into his chest
so my screams become muffled.
A button presses hard into my cheek,
and I can taste the old wool of his coat.
I stop yelling and close my mouth.

But my feelings can't be pushed down
inside of me anymore
after so many months of being brave.
I just can't keep quiet.

"I don't want to die, Papa," I sob.
"I don't want to die!"
Papa holds me for another minute,
and then he says,

"I will hide here with you."

He releases me and picks up the shovel again.
Dig. Toss. Dig. Toss.
I stop crying and watch
the hole grow longer.

Papa drops the shovel and steps into the hole.
Then he lies down in it.
"See?" he says.
"It's not so bad."

Hiding
I climb in and lie down beside him.
I turn on my side.
The hole is deep enough so that I cannot
see out over the edge.
It is just deep enough to hide a person
or two.

Papa puts his hand on my shoulder.
"Okay, my little girl," he whispers.
And then we don't talk.
The only sound I hear
is the beating of my heart—
very fast,

then not as fast,
then slower.
After a while I listen for other noises,
but there is nothing.

It is very quiet in a cemetery
at night.

Scary Thoughts
My body is still, but my mind is racing.
I want my mother.
I want my doll.
I want to be anywhere except
lying in the dark,
cold dampness
of somebody's grave.

Even with Papa here, I am still afraid.
What if the Nazis know that a little girl
lives in our apartment,
and they say to Mother and Dora,
Where is the child?
Give us the child!
Then they get angry because I am not there.

What if the soldiers
come looking for me
and search and search
until they find Papa and me?
What if there really are
such things as ghosts
and dead people that walk around at night?

A Bed Fit for a King
After a while, I fall asleep.
When I wake up,
Papa is snoring gently.
I roll out carefully from underneath his arm
and lie on my back
in the hole.

First I see black,
then streaks of gray,
as the sky lightens and
night becomes day.

Papa sits up beside me.
"Good morning, Syvia," he whispers.
"What a fine night for sleeping

in this bed fit for kings."

I smile a little at his teasing.
"Can we go home now?" I whisper.
"Can we?"
"Don't move," says Papa,
not answering my question.
He slowly,
quietly,
pulls himself up to standing
and looks around.

Plop!
Papa drops back down
into the hole.

"Not yet, Syvia," he says.
Then he tells me something I can hardly believe.
When Papa stands up,
he can see our building!
Our apartment window faces the wall
of the cemetery
and from this spot
he can see a white sheet in our window.

"That white sheet," Papa whispers,
"is a signal.
Your mother and I arranged that when
the Germans are nearby,
the sheet will be up.
When it becomes safe,
Mother will take the sheet down."

Papa says he chose this grave site
weeks ago.
But he prayed that he'd never
have to use it.

"No more talking now," says Papa.
"Now we wait."

Waiting

Brown dirt with tan and white flecks.
My right hand with fingernails that need trimming.
A black button on the wrist cuff
of Papa's wool coat.
A splinter in my left hand from the wooden
broom handle at home.
These are the things I can see while I am in the hole.

When I look down at the tip of my nose,
my eyes cross.
I can hold my breath to the count of forty.
The thread on my collar has unraveled
and needs to be stitched up.
A night and day can be a very long time.
These are the things I learn while I am in the hole.

Papa has checked from time to time all day long,
but still the sheet is up.
Then, just as the sun begins to set . . .

"Syvia! Syvia!"
It's Dora! I hear her voice, not far away!
Papa leaps up.
The sheet is down!
I can get up now.
There is Dora, searching the graveyard.

"Syvia! Papa!" Dora runs over.
"I couldn't wait! The Germans are gone.
Mother said I could come tell you."

I am safe.

I am stiff.
I am sore.
But I am safe.

"Come on," Dora says.
"This place gives me the shivers."

The Others
Look! Over there!
From behind a gravestone not too far away,
a boy walks out.
And there's a little girl holding
the hand of a woman
as they crawl out from behind another stone.

On our way back home,
we pass a few other children and grown-ups.
All that time they were hiding, too.
All that time, we were not alone.

Dora's shouting has let them know, too,
that it is safe to come out.
Safe.
At least for one more day.

While We Were Hiding

The soldiers came to our apartment and searched
even under the bed.
Then, without a word to Mother or Dora,
they thundered out the door
and on to the next family.
But they remained in the neighborhood
through the night
and into the next day.
They searched and smoked cigarettes on the street
and laughed loudly
and sometimes took away children,
then returned for more.

"I thought they'd never go away," Dora says.
"I hope they never come back," I say.
But Papa says that his sources tell him
that the Nazis plan to return
again and again
until they are completely sure
all the children are
gone.

"So Syvia and I may be spending some more time

together under the stars," Papa tells us.

He is trying to be funny, I know,
because there were no stars in the night sky.
Only a smoky haze
from the factories.

Good Ears
"What are sources?" I ask Papa later.
"You said sources tell you things about the Nazis.
Perhaps these sources are mistaken!"

"Sources are people with good ears," says Papa.
"And I can trust them to tell me information
that is correct."
Oh.
I think, *maybe I can be a source when I get older.*
I have good ears.
I often hear the neighbors arguing
through the walls,
and once I heard Papa whisper to Mother
all the way across the apartment
that she was a magnificent cook.
But then again,

maybe it's sometimes not so nice
to have good ears, because
I just heard the train whistle
and now I'm thinking about all the children
who were rounded up last night
by the soldiers.
The children who are now on that train.

I cover my ears with my hands
to make the sound
of the whistle
go away.

More Nights

There are more nights
in the cemetery
for Papa and me,
until the Nazis learn that it is a hiding place.

"Run!" Papa tells me the night the Nazis come,
and together we flee from our hole,
over the fence,
back to the street.
"What luck," says Papa,

"that the soldiers are searching
the other side of the graveyard first."

We have time to find a stairwell leading to a
basement apartment
on a small side street.
No one finds us there.

Now Papa scouts out new places to hide
during the day,
while he makes his rounds for work.
We have been escaping to those places
during the night
while the Nazis swarm the neighborhoods.

Stairwells.
Alleys.
Tight corners and cramped nooks.

Papa and I learn to doze off
in the most uncomfortable of circumstances.
That's what he calls our nights out.

"Are you ready for the most uncomfortable of

circumstances?" Papa will ask me.
Mother does not approve of his joking at times like
these.
So he always says it after we are out the door.

Before we leave, everyone acts serious.
We all know, without saying it out loud,
that Papa and I may not come back.
But every night for weeks we go out,
and Papa makes a little joke.
And the next morning we return back to our family.
Safe.

The Little Dance
The Nazis have made a new announcement:
No more nighttime searches!
No more deportations!
That is the good news.
When I hear it, I do a little dance.

Hop, skip, twirl.
No more hiding outside.
Hop, skip, twirl.

No more scary darkness—
I can sleep in a bed
with both my parents tonight!
Hop, twirl, bow.

Then I hear the bad news,
and my dance
is
done.

The Bad News
The searches and deportations
are over
because all of the children
are gone.

All of them?

The ghetto is a cage
holding parents wild with grief,
and all that can be done is
wait and hope and pray
that the Nazis are right,
that the children are in a better place.

Dora says that at the factory she, too,
must pretend to be very sad
because no one knows that her sister
is still here.
Everyone thinks that the soldiers found
all the boys,
all the girls,
all the babies,
and took them away.

All of them?

"Almost all," Papa says.
"Mama's sister Rose has her daughter, Mina,
hidden in the ghetto.
My brother Haskel's wife, Hana, has not had the
baby yet, so it is safe.
And, of course, there is Syvia.
We must hope that there are others."
But his brow turns down
as he says this.
"Mama's other sisters are not so lucky.
Sara and Shmuel's two boys are gone."

I hope they will be all right.

Too Quiet
Dora says it is strange
to walk through the streets
and not see a single child
or hear one baby.

I do not know what it is like.
I am not allowed outside
in daylight anymore,
even with my family.

The New Rules
These are the rules:
No one must see Syvia.
No one must hear Syvia.
No one must know that she is here.
She must stay inside the apartment
at all times.
She must not play loudly or shout,
and she must stay away from the window unless the
curtain is down.

"For how long?" I ask Papa,
trying to sound brave.

"Until . . .
Until . . ."
Papa pauses and looks at the ceiling
as if the answer to my question is
up above us.

Finally he tells me he just doesn't know the answer,
that these days we cannot plan the future
but instead must go day to day,
trusting that there will be an end to this situation,
that a better life is ahead.

Later, I think about what Papa has said.
I try to picture a better life.
It is hard to do,
since I have known this one for so long.
I squeeze my eyes shut
and see on the inside of my eyelids
a big meal of meat and potatoes and milk
and shiny shoes that fit me
and a red bicycle with a basket and a little bell.

Yes, I will learn to ride a bicycle
in this better life,
I think.
Maybe I'll even go fast.

Talks with Dora

Dora feels bad for me
having to stay inside all the time,
so she brings home funny stories and jokes
to cheer me up.
We sit together on her bed in the evening
and talk.
She tells me about the factory.
Now they are making munitions.
Bullets and weapons
for the Nazis to win the war.

The Nazis want to take over the world,
Dora believes.
They think that they are better than everyone else,
and they especially hate the Jews.

"Why do they hate us so much?" I want to know.

I have asked this before, but maybe
I'll understand better,
now that I'm older.
"They think we killed their God," replies Dora.

This makes little sense to me,
because no one I know ever killed anyone.
Then I become worried.

"God is dead?" I say.

"Not our God, *their God*," Dora says.
I'm still confused but I'm relieved.
God is still alive.

Then I have a new worry.
If God dies, who will run the world?
I hope it's not the Nazis.
I want to ask Dora about this,
but she has fallen asleep.

Games
Games I play to pass the time:

#1—"Different Views"
To play this game, I lie down in various
parts of the apartment
and stare at the different views.
Sometimes I lie on my back,
sometimes on my side,
sometimes on my stomach.

My favorite view is of the shoes lined up
at the door.
My least favorite is from under the bed.
Too dark.

#2—"Dust Dolls"
I make families out of balls of dust.
There is always a mother and a father
and lots of children.
The smallest piece of dust is the baby.
I gently blow to make the people move.
I feel a little guilty at the end of this game,
when I have to sweep them up.

#3—"Lessons"
At night I ask Dora to teach me

things, like adding and subtracting
and spelling,
and the next day I practice the lesson
over and over in my head.

I like my games,
but I wish I had somebody else to play them with.

Part Four

By 1943, the residents of the Lodz ghetto had heard the rumors about Nazi extermination camps. Most did not believe Rumkowski's reassurances that everything was under control. Rumkowski kept telling the Jews that they were necessary to the Nazis as long as they continued working and producing. There were ninety-six factories in the Lodz ghetto, with more than seventy thousand workers. Most of the factories produced textiles. Some built munitions.

The men and women in the ghetto tried to convince themselves that their work really was essential, that the Nazis would not harm them.

In the Lodz ghetto, some people tried to form an underground group to fight back against the Nazis. But it was impossible to organize anything effective.

In the capital city of Warsaw, however, resistance was more successful. After watching the population of the Warsaw ghetto dwindle from 350,000 to less than 35,000, some of the remaining Jews fought back. They held uprisings and used guns and homemade bombs. For the first time in the war, Jews killed Germans. The German troops, of course, retaliated. In April 1943, German soldiers set the ghetto on fire and watched it burn. Many Jews burned to death, and others were shot by the Nazis as they tried to escape.

The tale of the Warsaw ghetto heroics spread to the residents of Lodz. They quietly cheered the brave Jews who had fought back, even as they mourned the deaths of so many.

✡ WINTER 1942–SPRING 1944

Almost Two Years Go By
Days and days of hiding
turn into weeks
and then months.
Each day seems the same,
except for the weather.
It changes with the seasons.
Sometimes it is freezing cold in our apartment,
and sometimes it is boiling hot.

Another Ghetto
Sometimes I forget there are other people
outside our ghetto.

Dora says that in another city, our capital city,
there is a ghetto
even larger than ours.
It is the Warsaw ghetto,
and something incredible is happening there.
Jews are fighting back.

Dora says there have been uprisings
by Jews with stolen guns, bombs, grenades.

They have killed some soldiers!
Dora calls them resistance fighters
who make their plans "underground."

I imagine them like ants
tunneling through the ground
with guns.
But then Dora explains it's not that kind
of underground.

Still, I can't help but wonder what's going on
under the ground of Lodz.
Dora says, not much.

Growing Girl
I grow taller
and skinnier.
Mother frets that I am all bones,
but she is just as thin.
There is little food,
and a number of times we come close to starving.
It is kind of like sleepwalking
to live life in the ghetto.
We are all weak,

and our brains are foggy.

A little while ago they changed the rules again.
One child now allowed per family.
The Nazis perhaps
could not keep track of all the new babies
being born,
so they decided not to bother,
and, of course, they think
there are no older children left.

The new rule
did not change things much, though,
because Mother says it is
too dangerous
for me to go outside anyway.
Too much filth, sickness, sadness,
but it feels a little nice
to know that if I did step outside,
I wouldn't be
breaking the rules.

I have my eighth birthday while in hiding
and then my ninth.

Time goes on,
and so do we.

Part Five

*By mid-1944, all of the ghettos—except for Lodz—had
been destroyed. Rumkowski repeated that Lodz had survived because of the ghetto's hard workers. But then, the
Nazis asked for volunteers to help clean up cities in
Germany that had been bombed. While the Jews in Lodz
were suspicious of this request, the Nazis made it seem
legitimate. Volunteers lined up at the train station, and
soldiers carefully checked their luggage, assuring the men
and women they would get their belongings back at the end
of the journey. The soldiers also apologized for the uncomfortable method of travel. Freight cars, they explained, were
the only transportation not being used to fight in the war.*

*By July fifteenth, 7,175 "volunteers" had taken the
trains . . . to Chelmno extermination camp, where they
were killed.*

*Then began liquidation. The Nazis ordered the Lodz
ghetto to be emptied of people. This time there was no
request for volunteers, no checking of baggage. From August
27 to August 30, the residents of Lodz were transported out*

of the ghetto in crowded freight trains. Their destination was Auschwitz-Birkenau, where crematory ovens burned twenty-four hours a day. When the last train departed, 74,000 persons had already been sent to Auschwitz. Among the last to go were Rumkowski and his new wife, who were gassed to death.

Approximately 1,200 Jews were left behind in the ghetto to clean it up.

Outside the ghetto, war raged on. On June 6, 1944, the Allies stormed the beaches of Normandy, France, a day known as D-day. The Allies were on their way to winning the war in Europe.

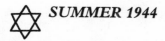 **SUMMER 1944**

Losing the War
Into the silence
of thousands of weak, weary Jews,
comes a shock wave:
The Germans are losing the war!
Papa says it is true.
I repeat the words over and over to myself.
The Germans are losing the war.

I cannot imagine who could beat
the Nazis.
They are so big and so powerful
with so many guns,
but Papa says the British and Soviets
and Americans
are even stronger.

I picture their soldiers
as giants.
Papa says no, they are just very brave,
regular-sized men.
"I'll bet the Americans look like movie stars."
Dora sighs,

and for a moment I remember the
old Dora,
who was popular and happy
and talked about boys.

Now I look at my
thin, weary sister
and I say,
"Yes, movie stars,"
even though I've never seen a movie
in my whole life.

What Next?
What happens to us if the Germans lose the war?
We will go home, I hope.
All the people,
like Hava and Itka and the others,
will come back to Lodz, too,
I hope.

I keep on hoping,
even though Dora says that some people
believe that the Jews
who left the ghetto

won't be coming back.

I'm not a little child anymore.
I know that she means
they might be dead,
not just in another place somewhere,
but it doesn't make sense
that all those people
are dead.
It's impossible.

Another Question
Here is another question.
There are Russians and British and Americans
(and people called 'Stralians)
who are coming to rescue the Polish people.

But what about the Jews?

If even people of our own country
did not try to help us
when we were put into the ghetto,
why would these foreigners
want to save us?

It is very lonely being Jewish,
I think.
And confusing.

Shipping Out
An announcement from Rumkowski,
leader of the Jews.
The Nazis need workers to go into Germany
and help repair damages
caused by the enemy.

Ghetto residents are to be shipped out
by train.

This week, the first trainloads
pull out of the station.
The trains carry all the people from the hospitals.
And this is very worrisome.
It doesn't make sense that
the sickest and the frailest
would be chosen to fix Germany!

Papa has heard that
door-to-door searches

and round-ups
will be starting again.
When the Nazi soldiers come
to our neighborhood this time,
I'm afraid I will be too tired
to run.

It seems unfair to wait for years
for the war to end
so that we can decide about the rest of our lives
and now that it may be ending,
the Germans will decide what to do
with us.

A Knock on the Door
At night there is a knock on the door.
It's my Uncle Hyman!
It is rare to see anyone
besides Papa, Mother, and Dora.
I want to say hello!
but my uncle did not come for hellos.
His daughter, Mina, has been taken by soldiers,
and he needs Papa's help.

Out the door in a flash
goes Papa,
and we wait
all night
for him to come back.

Search
Early the next morning,
Papa returns,
and we sigh with relief,
because he says everyone is safe.

This, Papa says, is what happened.
The soldiers blocked off the streets
surrounding our relatives' neighborhood
and searched every building.
They pulled Mina
right out of Aunt Rose's arms
and took her away.

So Mina's father, Hyman,
came to our apartment because
(and Papa says this briskly,
as if it is not a big thing)

many people
who like Papa and respect him
owe him favors.
That's why Uncle Hyman
thinks he can help.

So Papa and my uncle went out
and woke people
and asked around
and learned that the captured were taken
to a ghetto hospital
to be held overnight
before being deported in the morning
on an early train.

Papa, through his sources,
obtained two outfits
worn by chimney sweepers,
and a wheelbarrow.
Next the two men went to Papa's workplace
and took some bags of flour
and filled the wheelbarrow.
Then they went to the hospital.

Rescue

No one even gave them a second look
as they went in.
"I planned to say, 'Here to sweep the chimneys,'"
Papa tells us,
"but no one even asked."
So the men looked in the rooms,
and guess what they found?
Three children!
One of them was my cousin Mina!

Hide in the wheelbarrow, they told her,
under the flour sacks.
Then they calmly wheeled her out
of the hospital
to a safe hiding place.
And then
they went back in two more times
to carry out the other children.

"Now all three children
are back home with their families,
asleep," says Papa,
"and you should be, too.

Back to bed, Dora, Syvia.
Good night."

"It is morning,"
I point out.
"Go to sleep," says Mother,
And I do.

Liquidation

Papa and Mother are at work,
but Dora has the day off.
She is very quiet,
so I ask her, "What is the matter?"

"They are emptying out the ghetto," she responds.
"The Nazis. They are packing everybody
they can find
onto trains
and sending them away."

Trainloads and
trainloads and
trainloads
of people,

until there is nobody left.
Even Rumkowski,
the "leader of the Jews."
He got married not long ago,
and people complained
that he got special treatment.
So much fuss over his wedding
when so many were suffering.
But in the end,
there was no special treatment,
even for Rumkowski.
He got stuffed into a train car
like a regular Jew.

Aunt Sara and Uncle Shmuel—gone on the trains.
Aunt Rose and Uncle Hyman and, yes, Mina.
On the trains.
Malka. Edit, Esther, and Sura. Gone, too.

"It is only a matter of time,"
Dora says,
"before it is our turn."

In the Moonlight
Nighttime.
The moon casts a beam down,
joining its light with the lanterns
carried by Nazi soldiers
marching through the streets
on their way
to our apartment.

It Is Time
The soldiers stomp through our building.
Walls shake,
windows rattle,
my body trembles,
and we all are awake, knowing
the time has come.

"Everybody out! Everybody out!"
Pound! Pound! Pound!
This time "everybody"
includes my family
and me.
We all dress silently.
My hands shake with fear,

and I cannot button my dress,
so Mother helps me.
Papa opens the door and steps out
into the hallway.
Dora takes my hand and we follow.
Mother comes out behind us
and shuts the door.
We stand in the hall.
What else are we to do?
Papa is a strong man,
but even he can not fight off
soldiers with guns.

Other men and women come out
of their apartments,
some half-asleep, rubbing their eyes.

And then
the soldiers appear and herd us down the stairs
and outside,
where many other Jews
and many other soldiers
are walking down the street.
We are ordered to step in with the group.

We start walking.
Papa and Mother.
Dora and me between them.
One family
among hundreds
being swept along with the tide,
a sea of innocents simply
following orders
as dawn breaks
and the sun begins to rise.

Moving Forward

I should be frightened
but at the moment all I feel is
squashed
between bodies—
everyone so thin!—
as we move forward.
My legs are wobbly
because I haven't walked this far
in a long, long time.
There is a shout from behind us
and a gunshot.
A woman cries out, "Oh, no!"

but we keep moving forward.
I can't see anything
except the back of the man ahead of me.
Dora squeezes my hand
from time to time
and then the crowd stops moving.
A Nazi has yelled,
"Jews, halt!"

Front of the Line
We stand in a line,
Papa first,
then Dora and me,
then Mother,
waiting for a minute,
then moving a few steps forward.
Stopping, moving,
until, after about an hour,
Papa is at the front of the line
facing a group of German soldiers.
Dora steps in front of me.
"Next!" a soldier shouts.
Papa walks up to the Nazis.
I peer around my sister's back to watch.

I see Papa lift a large bag and toss it onto
his shoulder.
The soldiers nod and point to the right,
where a small group of men and women stand.
Papa nods back and waves to us, *come.*

Dora, Mother, and I walk quickly to the right
toward Papa.
Then a shrill whistle blows.
"Nein!"
The soldiers look at me with hard, angry faces.
"Nein!"
My heart is pounding,
my mouth is dry.
What?
What do I do? Or say?
The Nazis are all looking at me.
I feel dizzy.
Soldiers with guns,
are pointing at me,
speaking words I do not understand.
Then Papa leaves the group to the right
and meets me and takes my hand.
The Nazis wave Dora and Mother and Papa and me

to the left,
where there is a very large crowd
of hundreds of people.
We join them.

Announcement
The loudspeakers crackle.
Zzkrrch!
Then a man's voice announces:
"All Jews except those on the list must report to the train station
tomorrow morning at seven.
Each Jew may bring one bag.
Repeat . . .
all Jews except those on the list must report . . .''

I press my hands against my ears
to drown out the sound.
I bury my face in Papa's coat,
shrinking away from the crowd of tall bodies
that is buzzing with the Nazis' orders.
I close my eyes and hide until
Dora pulls one hand away from my ear.
"It's time to go home,"

she says.

So Papa, Mother, Dora, and I
return to the apartment
for one last night.

"What is the list?"
I ask Dora while we are trudging up the stairs
of our apartment building.
"It is a list of the names of the people that the Nazis
are keeping behind
in the ghetto," Dora tells me.
"They need some Jews to stay here
and clean up."

"Who is on the list?"
I ask Dora while we are climbing into our beds.
"The strongest and healthiest men and women,"
says Dora.
"Those were the people who were sent
to the right side."
"But Papa was sent to the right side!" I exclaim.
"Is he on the list?"
Dora sighs.

"Syvia, remember when Papa lifted that
one-hundred-kilogram bag of flour?
He proved to the soldiers that he was
strong and healthy.
So, yes, his name would have been added to the list,
and Mother and I could have cleaned up, too.
We are very lucky to not be ill."

I look at my thin, tired sister
and realize what a miracle it is
that my family is not sick
or dead
like so many of the others.

"But we were not put on the list also?"
My voice is small as I ask the question.
I already know the answer
deep down.
"No," replies Dora.
"Papa says he would stay only if all of us
were put on the list.
'A family stays together,' he told the soldiers."

"And they did not want me on the list," I say.

"They did not want you,"
Dora echoes.
"No children on the right side.
I'm sorry, Syvia. That's just the way it is."

So all of us—Papa, Mother, Dora, and I—
were sent to the left together.

Right side stays.
Left side . . .
Trains.

Papa's Gut
Papa's gut is speaking to him.
That's what he told us.
"My gut says we should not go
to the trains."

"But, Isaac," Mother says,
"we have no choice.
And maybe they are telling us the truth—
that the trains will take us to a place
where we will have work."

Papa shakes his head.
"I have trusted my gut two times before,
and each time those feelings
have been right."

"Oh, Isaac," says Mother,
folding a dress into a small package
to tuck into a corner of her suitcase.
"Listen to reason,
not your stomach."

Bad Dreams
I am dreaming
that I am on a ship
sailing on stormy seas.
The boat rocks violently with the waves,
rolling to its left side,
to its right side,
to its left side.
In this dream I somehow know that
I am the only one
who can save the ship,
but I am so small
and the waves are so big!

I run to the top deck
and grab a wheel to try to steer the boat to safety,
but it is too heavy and slippery
and it spins out of my hands.
"I'm sorry!" I scream,
as the salty sea spray slaps my face.
"I'm sorry!
It's all my fault!"

"I'm sorry! It's all my fault!"
I am shaken awake suddenly,
back in bed
between my parents.

My tongue tastes tears.
I open my eyes.
It is dark, I cannot see,
but I can feel my mother's cool hand
stroke my forehead.
"Shhhh," she says.
Papa is awake also.
"Syvia," he whispers fiercely,
"it is *not* your fault.
It is the fault of the Nazis.

You are to blame for nothing."

As my tears dry up
and Mother shushes me back to sleep,
I almost believe him.

Decision
The next morning,
my family walks through the streets,
carrying suitcases
with hundreds of other people,
everyone moving in the same direction.

"Isaac!"
A shout.
It is my father's brother Haskel!
And, look, there is my uncle's wife, Hana!
And baby Isaac,
who is not really a baby anymore
but a little boy of three.
My aunt carries him in her arms.

Papa and my uncle stop in the middle
of the crowd and talk,

their hands and mouths moving quickly.
My uncle goes to his wife and speaks to her,
then ruffles my little cousin's hair
and dashes ahead through the crowd.

"Let's go,"
Papa says to us,
and my family
and my uncle's wife and child
follow Papa.
He makes a turn away from the crowd,
away from the direction of the train station,
and toward his gut feeling.

The Plan
The Nazis are busy in the
thick, thick crowd.
People are milling everywhere,
so the soldiers don't notice
one small family
quietly leave.

We are going to the workers' houses,
Papa explains as we try to keep up with

his long legs.

"But we are not on the list!"
Mother and Dora say aloud.
These are the words I am thinking, too,
but do not say because I am concentrating
on making my legs move faster,
so I can catch up to Papa
and hold his hand.

"Over there are the houses where
the workers will live."
Papa ignores all talk of lists
and points toward some buildings.
"Syvia, you wait here with baby Isaac."
He waves at the women to follow him
to the buildings.

"We will act as if we are workers,
and, after we are settled inside,
I will return for the children."
Papa speaks confidently,
and if there are any doubts about this plan,
no one voices them.

Baby-sitting

So here I am
with my cousin Isaac,
standing behind a big tree.
I am not used to being outside
with no grown-ups around,
not even any soldiers,
and now I am the older one
for the first time in my life.

"Would you like to see
what I have in my case?"
I ask.
Baby Isaac blinks at me.
He has huge brown eyes.
He doesn't say anything.
I realize later that he has learned to be
very, very quiet
so as not to disturb anyone,
especially Nazis.
He sits down and watches me
open my case.
He is not interested much
in the clothing,

but he likes the *thwap* of the lid
when I open and shut my suitcase.

So that is how we spend our time.
Opening and closing, *thwap!*
Opening and closing, *thwap!*

Then Isaac lies down on the ground
and closes his eyes
and falls asleep.

Patience
It seems like an awfully long time
since my family left.
The ghetto is a different world
without all the people in the streets.
I can hear noises off in the distance,
but around me it is quiet,
too quiet.
My thoughts keep interrupting
the silence
with their noise.
What if the Nazis have caught my papa,
my mother,

my sister,
and taken them to the trains
or worse yet, shot them on the spot?
Then I'd be left behind,
wondering what happened,
maybe never finding out.
I cannot just stay here forever with Isaac,
but Papa said don't move,
wait here.

More unwanted thoughts creep into my brain—
things I have tried to forget.
I once saw a man
being killed
out on the streets.
Bang! Bang!
A man in the crowd did a funny jump,
then fell on his back,
his yellow star facing the sky.
Other people jumped, too,
away from the man,
then kept walking, faster,
and Dora tugged me away
so I couldn't see anymore.

I look down at my cousin sleeping.
Then I look toward the buildings
where the workers will stay.
Is that a person coming?
It is hard to tell from this far away, but then . . .
Papa?
Papa?
Papa!

My papa comes to me,
and he is grinning.

Papa!
He is here!
He is safe!
I want to dance and hug and ask questions,
but Papa puts his finger to his lips and says,
"Shhh . . . let Isaac sleep.
It will be easier that way."
He scoops up baby Isaac
and lays him over one shoulder.
Next he tosses his coat over Isaac
to hide him.
Then he takes my hand.

His hand feels strong and safe,
covering my small fingers,
and, as we walk together, Papa talks softly.
I listen and
Isaac sleeps on.
One little boy is not too heavy, I think,
for a man who can lift
a one hundred-kilogram bag of flour.

And then fool the Nazis.

Entrance
This is what happened.
Papa, Mother, Dora, Aunt Hana, and Uncle Haskel
walked up to the entrance of one of the buildings
where some men and women had just entered.

Nazi soldiers guarded the door.
Papa looked right into the eyes of one of the soldiers.
"Isaac Perlmutter," he said,
then announced the others' names,
pointing to each one by one.

The soldier looked them all over

and nodded.
The other soldier opened the door,
and Papa, Mother, Dora, Aunt Hana,
and Uncle Haskel
went in to join the workers.

How Papa Knew
"That is the whole story?" I asked, amazed.
"What about the list? How did you know the
soldiers wouldn't shoot you?"

"It is true that the warnings said
that everyone who did not
report to the trains would be shot,"
Papa admits,
"but I could not bring myself to do it.
My gut insisted, do not go to the trains."

"Did your gut talk to you about the list, too?"
I ask.

"No," Papa chuckles,
"for that I used my two eyes.
I have noticed that lately

there have been fewer and fewer
soldiers around in the ghetto,
because Germany needs its men
for fighting.
Hitler does not have the time these days
to concern himself with
one ghetto
of Jews
when the world is coming after him.

"So, I realized that there might not be enough
soldiers left here
to be organized with this liquidation,
and yesterday when I was lifting
that bag of flour,
I looked around and saw . . . nothing."

"Nothing, Papa?" I trotted alongside him.
We were getting closer to the buildings now.

"I saw that not one soldier
had pen and paper
to take names,
and today at the entrance I saw again nothing.

No paper, no pens,
no list."

"There was no list!" I could not believe it.
Was *everything* the Nazis said lies?

"Only soldiers with guns." Papa smiles.
"And I am pleased to say
that they did not use them."

Into the Building
When we approach the two buildings
where the workers will live,
Papa says,
"Walk on my right side, Syvia,
and keep your head down."

We walk up a path made of dirt and stones.
I watch my shoes, step . . . step,
and just for a moment I can't help but
lift my head.
Out of the corner of my eye, I see
two German soldiers.
They are talking to a woman

who looks upset.
She is waving her arms around
while she speaks to the men.

Papa still carries baby Isaac over his shoulder,
and I walk close so that Papa's body will
block me from the soldiers' view.
But the soldiers are busy arguing with the woman,
and they don't even look our way.
I can hardly believe how risky this plan is.
How brave Papa is.
How lucky we are.

Around to the side of one building we go!
Two children and one man—
who were not even on "the list"—
through a side door,
down a stairway,
into a cellar.

The Underground Room
I've never really thought about what cellars are like.
We did not have one when we lived on the second
floor of the apartment,

but one look, and I know
this is not an ordinary cellar.

Children.

There are children in this cellar.
It is dark, so I don't know for sure,
but it looks like maybe five,
maybe six
girls and boys
are sitting on suitcases or on the floor.

Baby Isaac wakes up just then.
He looks around and cries out, "Mama?"
"It's all right, Isaac." Papa hushes the boy.
"Your mama and papa will be here soon."

A hundred thoughts bubble up in my head.
Isaac's mother and father will be here?
Where are my mother and Dora?
Am I to stay here in a room under the ground?

"Others!" I say, my voice too loud
for this silent room.

"There are *other* children still alive in the ghetto!"

Papa nods.
He says,
"They have been hidden, too.
We can talk more about it later,
but for now I need you to stay here
and get settled in.
Take care of your cousin."
Papa puts baby Isaac down
and pushes him gently toward me.
I need to take care of unfinished business
out there."
Papa points to the exit door
leading to the stairwell.

"Where are you going, Papa?" I cry out.
He's leaving me again?
"Don't worry, Syvia," Papa says.
"I will return, I promise,
and you will see your mother and sister
again very soon."

So I watch Papa leave

as I hold a small hand
and a suitcase.

After he is gone,
I take a deep breath and turn around,
staring at the others.

Children of the Cellar
"Hello,
my name is Syvia.
I am nine years old."

This is what I would like to say.
It is what I would say
if I were someone like Dora,
who always knows the right words
around other people
and is not afraid to say them.
But I am not brave,
I am shy,
so instead I feel my cheeks burn,
and I look down at the floor.

"Come, Isaac," I whisper,

and I drag my cousin and my suitcase
over to the corner of the cellar
that is darkest,
and we sit down on the floor
to wait.

No one else is talking
or moving.
I feel quite alone in the cool, dark
silence of this cellar.

The door to the outside opens
three times.
Each time I catch my breath,
expecting to see someone from my family.
But each time it is a strange adult,
dropping off another lost-looking child.
I squint and count
ten others
besides Isaac and me.

My family should be here soon.
If Dora comes first, I will run to her
and hug her.

The other children will look over.
No one can replace Hava or Itka
as my best friends,
but perhaps we will all get along well enough?
We already have one thing in common.
We are all children of the cellar.

Children of the cellar.

For some reason,
this thought strikes me as Very Important,
and I make a note in my head to tell it to Dora
when she comes.

"Syvia," my little cousin's voice breaks
into my daydreams.
"You look funny."

I try to tell Isaac that
that is not a nice thing to say,
but my tongue seems not to be working
and my head has a buzzing inside it.
The room begins to tilt,
then everything

goes
black.

Not Myself
My mother's face.
Papa!
Dora, what took you so long?
Red flowers.
What are flowers doing in the ghetto?
The dust family from our old apartment comes to life.
They sweep me with a broom.
Sweep, sweep, into a cellar
filled with dogs, big dogs,
staring at me with yellow eyes,
chanting my name, Syvia, Syvia.
Talking dogs?
I feel chilled, then hot, and I keep hearing,

"Syvia! Syvia! You're awake!"
It is Dora,
looking with anxious eyes
into my face.
I am lying down on the floor of the cellar,
a thin blanket underneath me.

I feel damp, sweaty.

"Mama? Papa?" I ask.
My throat is scratchy, I do not sound like myself.

"They are fine," says my sister.
"They are working right now,
but they have both been here to see you."

"Papa and Mother were here?"
Dora has given me a sip of coffee-water,
so I can speak more clearly now.

"Lots of times," Dora says.
"One of us has been here with you
so you wouldn't be afraid when you woke up."
"Was I sleeping?"
I don't remember falling asleep.
"In a way," Dora tells me.
"You fainted."
"I did?"
I'm not even sure what fainting is, exactly.
"When?"
"Three days ago," says Dora.

I take another sip.
And another.

A Little Tired
Three days ago,
Mother had come to the cellar,
Dora tells me.
At first Mother thought I was napping,
but when she tried to wake me up,
I wouldn't respond.
Then Papa and Dora came down.
Dora said she got scared,
I looked so still and pale,
but Mother fed me some vegetable broth
that she had brought for me in a dish.
I sipped it,
half-awake.

Papa and Mother
let me rest
and drink broth
and told Dora not to worry.
Once my fever broke,
I would be all right.

"How do you feel?" asks Dora.
"A little tired," I say,
"but not too bad."
Dora smiles, as if I've made her very happy.

Suddenly I remember—
Baby Isaac!
I was supposed to be watching him!
I look around the room
and see him
playing a hand-clapping game
with another boy.
"Isaac is fine," Dora assures me.
"He has even made a friend."

I want to get up and go to him,
but my legs feel too shaky
and it is hard to hold my head up.

"Tell me one thing, Dora," I say,
before sleep overtakes me again.
"Do the Germans know we are here?
Do they know that there are children here?"
"No." Dora shakes her head,

her dark hair brushing her cheeks.
"No, as far as the Nazis know,
there are eight hundred adults
and no children
left in the Lodz ghetto."

Well, then, aren't we clever,
I think as I drift off.
We know more than the Nazis do.

A Pile of Bones
Sleeping.
Sleeping.
I sleep a lot over the next few days.
Papa and some other men carry down
bedrolls of blankets
so no one has to sleep on the hard floor.

One would think a room full of children
would be noisy,
but it is mostly quiet.
After months and months of very little
food or sunlight,
we are weak and listless.

I feel like a pile of bones
lying in the corner.

This is not what it was like
when I played with Hava and Itka.
We had energy to have fun,
but now that we are children of the cellar,
we just lie around
or sit propped against a wall
and wait for the grown-ups to visit.

We all know how to hide,
to keep quiet so that the Nazis don't find us.

Even baby Isaac, the littlest one here,
plays quietly without fussing.
He naps on a blanket next to me.
I like to watch him sleep.
He breathes with his mouth open,
making a funny snuffling sound,
and when he has bad dreams,
I pat his head
and tell him everything is all right,
to go back to sleep.

Special Gifts

Family visits are a gift from above.
Mother brings me vegetable soup.
"The Germans keep lovely gardens," she tells me.
"And it is the women's job to pick the vegetables
for the soldiers' soup.
But we are also able to take some for ourselves."
The soup is thick and warm,
unlike the thin broth I am used to.
Mother comes twice a day with this soup,
and I feel a little stronger after every bowl.
Dora brings me little bits of outside.
Twigs, leaves, some berries—
not to eat, just to look at.
"The weather has been quite nice," she says.
"It makes the hard work almost pleasant."
Dora and the others have to walk
through the ghetto,
collecting the belongings of the people who were
sent to the trains—
furniture, clothing, personal items.
The workers must clean everything,
then it all goes to the Germans.
They won't have to clean anything from our apartment,

I think with some pride.
I kept everything very neat.

It is a treat when Mother and Dora visit.
But the very best part of the day
is when Papa comes.
He brings down stories,
and, when he talks, all the children listen
to his deep, kind voice.

How the Cellar Was Found
How did we children come to be in the cellar?
Papa explains:
"When I first arrived at these buildings,
I came inside and inspected each floor,
asking myself,
Where is a good hiding place?
Then I saw a door,
not easy to see unless you were really looking,
and I opened it.
There was a staircase going down! A cellar!

"Quickly I went back upstairs
and spoke to one of the workers,

a man that I knew from our old neighborhood.
After we spoke, this man walked out of the building
as if going about his new job.
He just walked by the soldiers, *la-di-da*,
humming a tune, so they wouldn't
suspect anything.
Then when he was far enough away,
he began running,
running, running,
toward the train station
to the mob of people getting on the trains.
"My friend says it was chaotic and noisy and
easy enough to blend into the large crowd,"
Papa tells us.
"What was not so easy was finding people
with children.
There were so few left.
But here and there, he'd spot one.

"Come," he said to a woman who was
holding a child by the hand.
"There is a place to hide the children
back in the ghetto."
The woman shook her head

no
and boarded the train.
Again and again the man approached adults
who had children,
and most of them said *no*,
but some said *yes*."

Yes or No
Papa continues talking.
Now all of the children are awake and listening.
"It must have been a difficult decision
for those people—
to get on the train
or stay behind.
Did they believe the trains were
going to a safe place
or did they think that anyone whose name was not
on the list
would be shot if he stayed?

"Or did they trust the stranger,
hot and sweaty from running,
enough to follow him back to the ghetto?

"We do not know where the people went who
chose the train,
but we do know that all of you
who turned around and came back
were smuggled in here
right under the Nazis' noses.

"And," Papa finishes his tale and grins at us,
"here you all are!"

How We Got Inside
"How did we all get in here
without the soldiers noticing?"
I ask.

"Sometimes it was too simple," Papa says.
"The soldiers were not always
guarding the building,
since their work habits have gotten so careless.
Other times,
we used the method of distraction."
"What is that?" asks baby Isaac.
He has stopped rolling around

a small ball of yarn to listen.

"One of the women would approach the soldiers
with a question,
turning the mens' attention away
from the buildings
so we could smuggle in the children,"
Papa explains.

"The woman arguing with the soldiers!" I say.
"I remember seeing her
when baby Isaac and I arrived!"
I also remember that Papa had told me
to keep my head down that time.

"Yes, Syvia." Papa doesn't seem angry;
in fact he laughs.
"That woman was quite the actress,
wasn't she?

"Many people worked together
to save you children.
We are blessed to have such good people
around us."

While I agree with Papa, I am also aware of
another blessing.

I am thinking how good it sounds
to hear Papa laugh.
It has been a long time
since I've heard laughter,
and it warms a place in my heart
that even the soup cannot touch.

Upstairs

Papa talks about what it is like
upstairs.
There is a building for the men
and a building for the women.
They are supposed to stay separated,
but someone found a secret door
connecting the two buildings,
so the men have been visiting
the women's building.
One person stands guard at the front entrance
and when the Germans approach,
the guard gives a signal
and all the men race back through the door
to their building.
"Like a pack of dogs running from the dogcatcher,"
says Papa.

The Germans check on the workers every so often.
But they rarely stay for long.
So Papa and Mother,
like the other men and women,
can spend some time together.
There are no tables,
so everyone sits on the floor to eat.
Like a big picnic, Papa says.

The best part is that the fruit
on the trees has ripened,
so everyone has the taste of sweet and juicy fruit in
their mouths.

Then Papa takes an apple out of his pocket and,
with a small knife,
he slices it up
and gives each of us children a piece.
I eat mine in small bites to make it last.
It is delicious.

The Ovens
In one part of the cellar is a large pile of coal.

The grown-ups use it to warm the ovens.
One morning Mother comes down to see me,
and I notice a red mark on the palm of her hand.

"Mother, did you hurt yourself?" I ask.
Mother looks at her hand and then at me.
Her mouth turns up in a small smile.

"Can you keep a secret, Syvia?"
Of course I can, I assure her.
So she tells me that there are
little electric ovens for cooking
upstairs in the kitchen.
The women use the kitchen to cook
for the Jewish workers.
The soldiers told the women,
No using the ovens!
Electricity costs too much money to
waste on Jews!
But the electric ovens work much faster
than the coal ovens
and instead of walking down and up stairs
carrying heavy coal,
all they have to do is flick a switch,

and the oven grows warm.

So, Mother tells me, the women have been using
the electric ovens
without the soldiers knowing.
They cook with the coal ovens,
but also the electric ones.
The soldiers just smell the food cooking
and think it's coming from the coal ovens only.
When the soldiers do come in,
which isn't often since the kitchen
is the women's place,
the women are prepared.

Mother was browning potatoes in a pan
when she heard the signal.
Germans!
Quickly she grabbed the handle
and hid the pan, potatoes and all,
under a bed.

"There was no time for a pot holder,"
Mother says,

"so the pan burned my hand.
But it does not hurt too much.
And the soldiers did not find out about the oven."

"What happened to the potatoes?" asks a voice.
I turn my head to see who is talking.
It is one of the boys.
He must have been listening, too.

"Unlike my hand . . ." Mother smiles again.
"The potatoes were unharmed.
In fact, you had some in last night's soup!"

It is so nice to have Mother smiling
and telling stories!
She is usually so serious, even stern.
I think that things must be not so bad upstairs.
The grown-ups seem to be in good spirits
these days.

Late Summer
Dora confirms my thoughts.
We are sipping soup together and talking.

"It is not so bad up there," she says,
"The weather is late-summer warm but not too hot
and food is more plentiful
than we have had in years.
It is like we are becoming humans again, Syvia.
Imagine!"

There is other good news.
The number of Germans appears to be dwindling.
The soldiers who remain seem more interested in
beer and liquor and cards
than in running the ghetto cleanup.
So the workers are mostly left alone,
not bullied or harassed like they used to be.

Dora pauses, slurps some soup, and surveys
my cellar surroundings.
She eyes the dingy walls and ceiling,
the dirty coal pile,
the children, unwashed except for hands and faces
which have had daily wipe downs by the women.

"It certainly does not seem like summertime

down here," my sister says.
"I wish I could bring you some sun, Syvia,
but the best I can do is soup."

The Chef
I still have not spoken to any of the other children.
I am having trouble even remembering who is who.
My brain cannot seem to hold on to names.
Isaac is the only child I feel comfortable with.
We play simple games like,
"Which hand is holding the stone?" and
"What color am I thinking of?"

Although I do not know the others,
I do get to know some things about them.
One little girl is weepy,
one boy is sickly,
another hates to get his face washed.

Then there is the boy who talks out loud
to himself
and his only subject is food.
This is what he sounds like—

Meat, stew, potatoes, peppers, roasted turnips, spices,
flour to thicken.
Cook over low heat.
Potato dumplings, edges browned, not burned.
Ladle thick gravy on roast.
Cabbage galumpkies, noodle kugel,
Carrot cake with dates, finely chopped . . .

In my head, I call this boy The Chef.

Papa says that thinking about food
all the time is not uncommon
among people in the ghetto,
who are around starving bodies.
The mind can latch onto nourishment in this way.
"People have different ways of surviving the days,"
Papa says.
"We must honor our differences while we
find our own courage and our own strength
the best we know how."

I think I understand what he means,
but, selfishly, I also wish

The Chef would keep his courage
to himself more often
and give us some peace.

Nervous Hands
Then there is the girl
whose right hand is always moving.
Open fingers, open hand,
close fingers, clench hand into a fist.
Open, clench, open, clench.
She even does this in her sleep.

I wonder why, and
if her hand gets tired.
Once I look at her and think,
It looks sort of like she is
shooting a gun,
but I don't like this thought.
It reminds me of a memory I have
that I never told anyone about.

When I was littler
I saw a soldier on the street.

I did not want to look at his face,
so I lowered my gaze
to his hand,
which was holding a pistol
straight out in front of him.
He pulled with his finger
and pop,
I think someone was killed
right then,
because I heard a cry and a thud
very close to where Dora and I were walking.
But it was not me or Dora
who got hit.
I never saw who it was.
One minute a person
is alive walking down a street,
then a hand moves a finger
and a person is dead.

Later I quietly tell Papa
about the girl who keeps opening and closing
her hand.
Papa says,

"I think, probably, she is the type of child
who needs to be moving.
Her body doesn't like to stay still.
It is just nervous energy."
He might be right,
but I look closer and I think,
She does not look nervous to me.
Her eyes look angry.
I decide to be careful around her,
just in case.
I think of her as Nervous Hands.

Mouse

Sometimes at night I cannot sleep,
and I have dark thoughts.
I feel lonely and scared and trapped
down in the cellar.
Papa says to "find our own courage,"
but I don't see any signs of
mine.

If I had a nickname,
it would be Mouse.

Brown and timid,
I burrow into the corner in my
nest of blankets.
I even sound squeaky
with my raw throat and lingering cough,
from the dampness of the cellar.
Yes, Mouse is a good name for me.
Hiding down here in my mouse hole,
I wait for yet another day.

Nobody Special

I have always been shy and quiet,
unlike other children with their lively games
and whoops and shouts.
Perhaps this is one reason
I am still here in the ghetto.
I know how to be invisible.

I am certainly no one special or important.
I'm just one plain brown-haired, skinny girl.
But I am alive and still here.
Am I lucky?
Surely not as lucky as children
who are not Jews.

But every day I get to be with
my parents and sister,
and in the ghetto that is
more than luck.
It is a miracle.

✡ *LATE FALL–WINTER 1944*

Pails of Coal

The grown-ups have asked us children
to carry pails of coal
up the stairs
to help out,
when soldiers are not nearby.
The pails are very, very heavy
when filled with coal.
After the first time I carried some pails up,
my hands felt sore
from where the metal handles
bit into my palms,
but my hands are getting used to it.

It feels good to be able to
help the grown-ups.
It feels good to be strong enough
to climb the stairs.

Blue Sky

So, over the past few days,
while the grown-ups have been out in the ghetto

working,
some of the children have gone upstairs
and outside.
So far nobody has been caught.
The soldiers don't come around
to the workers' houses
so much anymore.
I think it is very bold
of the children
to take such a chance,
but I can't help but notice how happy
their faces look when they come back.

I have a small scrap of fabric
that Dora found
and gave me.
It is pale blue.
It looks like the sky.

When the others return
from their adventures outdoors,
I take out my blue scrap
and look at
my sky.

But deep in my heart,
I know that it cannot replace the
real thing.

Up and Out
I am tired.
Tired of being inside this cellar.
Tired of being afraid.
Tired of being me.
I shove my blue scrap of fabric
into my shirt pocket
and put on my shoes.
They are too tight,
but I can still walk in them.
I get up and start walking.
Are these my *feet climbing up to the top of the stairs?*
Can this be my *hand pushing the door open?*

I go through the door,
out of the cellar,
into a little hallway.
There is another door.
I open it.
One hard push,

and I am outside.

I am outside!
The air smells so good, crisp like autumn,
not stale like cellar air.
For a minute I am blinded by the
sun.
My eyes adjust.
My heart goes *boomboomboomboom*.
I look around.
Nobody this way,
nobody that way.

There is a chill in the air.
The wind feels cold,
but the sun peeks out from behind clouds
and invites me out
into the yard.
I walk further outside,
feeling grass under my feet,
sunshine on my face.

There are trees in the yard.
Most of the leaves have dropped to the ground,

but not all have fallen.
And then I see it.
Hanging from a tree branch—
a large yellow pear.

Dora says that the workers are not
supposed to eat from the trees.
They are supposed to save the fruit
for the Germans,
while the workers get by on the food
the soldiers don't want.

My head is worrying, but
my feet are still walking.

The Pear
What if the Germans come into the yard?
What if they are looking out the window
of one of the buildings?
What if someone sees me?

I am drawn to the tree
like a bee to honey.
Closer.

Closer.
I can touch the tree branches now.

I reach up and grasp the pear.
Its skin is yellow green,
ripe.
I twist it a bit, and the pear
pops off its branch
into my hand.
It is solid, smooth,
real.

There is no stopping now.
At this moment there are no Germans,
no worries.
There is only me and this pear.
I take a bite.

Cool, juicy, sweet.
Perfect.
Delicious!

I eat some more.
My hand gets a little sticky,

but I don't care.
I am out in the sunshine
eating a pear,
just like any normal girl
who isn't Jewish in Poland,
on a regular day.

Suddenly I realize where I am,
what I am doing.
I had better get inside.
I am about to run back,
when I spot another pear on the tree,
a little smaller than my pear,
a little greener.
I think of Dora, and I grab it,
then turn and run
back to the building
with a pear in each hand.

Through the door,
down the hallway,
down the stairs,
into the cellar.

A Gift for Dora
I did it.
I made it.

Sitting cross-legged on my blanket,
I eat the rest of the pear,
nibbling around the seeds
and stem
until all that is left is the core.
The juice dries on my hand,
but I do not wipe it off,
saving the scent to sniff for a little while longer.

I put my hand up to my face.
Inhale.
Mmmm . . . perfume of pear.
Dora told me that rich and famous people
wear perfumes of
fruit and flowers.
Now, so do I.

Later, when Dora comes down to visit me,
I present her with
the small green pear,

wrapped in a piece of blue cloth
the color of sky.

Dora looks at me.
"You got this from Papa?"
I shake my head *no*.
"Mother?"
Again, no.

"I picked it for you myself," I say proudly.
Dora's face looks worried,
but only for a moment.
Then a smile breaks out.
"You went outside? By yourself?"
Dora laughs in delight,
and I laugh, too.
"Oh, Syvia," my sister says,
"what a clever and brave girl you are."

Clever and brave?

Me?
I guess I might be, after all.

"But, Syvia." Dora suddenly turns serious.
Oh no.
Is she going to scold me
for leaving the cellar?
For stealing?
What?
"You should get to eat the pear!"
She tries to give me the fruit.
"No, that is yours,"
I tell her.
I point to the leftover core
from my golden pear.
"I already ate mine."

This makes Dora laugh again.
Then she makes me share her pear.
Delicious,
we agree.

Heavy Boots
I want to tell baby Isaac
about my trip outside,
but he is napping.
I feel bad that I didn't save

some pear for him,
but I was so hungry,
I forgot.
Anyway, the grown-ups bring him special treats
because he is the youngest.
Still, I decide to give him the seeds.
We can make up a game
with them.

While I am thinking about seeds and pears,
I start to doze off.
I am awakened abruptly
by the sounds of heavy footsteps,
many of them
overhead.
Suddenly the door swings open.

Down the stairs come giant boots,
pant legs,
uniforms with swastikas!
The Nazis!
The Nazis are in the cellar!

Caught

All the children are awake now.
I am frozen.
The soldiers bark at each other,
but I don't know what they are saying.
Then one soldier grabs my arm
and yanks me up.

I feel like time slows down.
I can see my pear cores
lying on my blanket
like small skeletons.
I see scared faces,
my cousin Isaac's wide eyes
I am being dragged up the stairs.
Other soldiers
are pulling children,
following closely behind me.
Boys and girls are screaming,
"Help!" "Mommy!" "No!"

I'm too scared to scream.
Too scared to do anything
but be dragged like a sack of potatoes.

The Nazi pulls me by my arm,
kicks open the door,
and shoves me through it.

I fall and land on hard ground.
We are all outside now
in the hands of the Nazis.
Hands that are big and rough
and . . . *ow* . . .
pulling me up by my hair
so I am standing.

Captured
This is it.
This is the end.
I know what happens to people who
trick the Nazis,
who try to hide,
who refuse to give in.
I know what happens to Jews.

I am one little girl!
I want to yell at the soldiers.
You are big men with guns!

What could I possibly do to you?
Why can't you just leave us alone?
Papa!
Mother!
Dora!

The soldier grabs my arm and drags me forward.
I whimper
and shut my eyes.
If the Nazis are going to kill me,
I don't want to see them do it.

The Circle
The Nazi pulling on my arm suddenly stops
and mutters something.
I stop moving and wait, eyes closed,
for more pulling,
for death.

Nothing happens.

Little ovals of light
dance around the insides of my eyelids.
I feel dizzy and sick to my stomach.

The waiting becomes too much to bear.
I open my eyes,
slowly
adjusting to sunlight.
We are just a few steps from the building.
The soldier is still holding on to me
but . . .

I cannot believe what I am seeing.
There before us,
in a half circle surrounding the doorway,
are the grown-ups.
So many grown-ups.
It could be all 800.
All of the Jews in the ghetto.

The soldier grips my arm and marches me
toward the crowd,
but no one steps back.
No one moves out of his way.
The soldier turns his head and barks
something at the other Nazis
behind us.

The crowd stands as one,
looking at me
and the Nazi soldier.
I see a few women crying quietly.
Then the crowd of Jews starts moving,
forming a circle
around soldiers and children.
The Nazis seem unsure of what to do.
Certainly they have guns,
but they are outnumbered by hundreds
of people.

The soldier holding me
says something
angrily.
Then he
kicks me,
kicks me,
kicks me again.
He pushes me, and
I stumble into the crowd,
into the arms of grown-ups.
The other soldiers release their grips
on the children,

and then all of the Nazis
shove their way
through the circle,
away from the Jews.
I stand, shaking and crying.
My parents are running to me,
and here comes Dora, too.
My family embraces me.
In the distance I hear
the roar of motorcycles.
The Nazis
are gone.

In This Moment
Later I am told
that someone had tipped off the Nazis,
informing them that there were children
in the cellar.
Who betrayed us?
No one knows.

Later I am told
that almost everyone came running
as soon as they heard

the children were in danger.
(Many did not even know we were there,
that any children were left.)

Later I understand what happened.
There would have been trouble
if the soldiers had taken the children.
Some say the soldiers were going
to shoot us children right there
on the spot,
but they realized
that would have caused total chaos
in the ghetto.
The grown-ups saved us.

Many of the grown-ups
who had protected us
were the parents
of children who had been put on the trains.
They were the parents
of children who got sick or had starved
and died.

The twelve of us,

in a way,
were their children, too.

Later I have time to think about these things
and wish I could have said
Thank you
and
I'm sorry your child couldn't be here, too,
safely encircled
for that moment.

But in that moment
all I could do was cry and tell myself,
I'm alive.
I'm alive.

Upstairs
A few days have passed
since the Nazis found us.

Now I get to be upstairs in the women's building.
No more cellar!
Why did the soldiers
allow us children to live?

At first I was happy to be spared,
but then I thought of how the Nazis
would surely return.

Baby Isaac, the girl with the nervous hands, the boy
who talks about food—
all of us are up here
with the grown-ups.
There is no furniture.
Just cots set up for sleeping.
No tables or chairs.
We eat sitting on the floor.
But I do not mind—it is better than the cellar.

Dora says that the Nazis
are leaving us here for now
because they need the grown-ups to obey orders,
to do their dirty work.
If they took the children away now,
the adults would rebel.
Enough is enough, the grown-ups say.
Harm the children and there will be trouble.
But Dora is worried
that the soldiers haven't come back.

It might mean
that the Nazis
know that we'll all be dead soon anyway,
so why bother.

Winter Is Coming
There is a broken window in this room.
Frost patterns etch the glass
around the hole.
Someone takes a blanket
and covers the window up.

The weather has turned sharply colder.
The women are anxious about
winter.
We have no heat,
no hot water,
little food.

The grown-ups' words keep worrying their way
into my mind.
Words like "survive another winter" and
"freeze to death" and
"starve."

Tossing and Turning

The Germans are losing the war
and the soldiers are pushing the workers to move
faster, faster,
finish cleaning out this ghetto!

It is snowing and cold and
I am having trouble sleeping.
I cannot stop thinking about the Nazi
who pulled me from the cellar,
who kicked me
but did not kill me.

I could be dead right now
or I could be taken away
on a train,
riding with the other children
and all the furniture and belongings that were
taken out of empty ghetto homes
and delivered to Germans
who say that nothing belongs to
Jewish people anymore.

Not even their own children.

I toss and turn on the cot,
until Dora kicks me
to make me stop.
Her kick is gentle, though, unlike that Nazi's
that gave me bruises.

 **WINTER 1945**

The Soldier's Story
I help Mother wash the dishes.
It is hard to get them clean
with only cold water.
My hands feel like ice.
Papa comes in
from his day's work
and tells Mother something
I cannot help overhearing.

Today a German soldier
who was drunk
came up to Papa and some other workers
and said,
"You Jews. You think you are so smart.
But not smart enough to know
that you are all going to be shot
in the cemetery.
Bang! Bang! Dead Jews just falling everywhere."

Then the soldier laughed and stumbled away.

Mother keeps rinsing a dish.
"Should we be worried, Isaac?"
she asks.
"I don't think so,"
Papa replies, scratching his beard.
"He was very drunk.
The men think he was lying,
just trying to provoke us."
Papa sees me and stops talking.

"How was your day, Syvia?"
he asks.
I say what I always say.
Fine, Papa.
And I pretend I did not hear
anything.

Two Large Holes
The next day everything turns upside down.
Very large holes.
That is what the Nazis
have told some of the men to
make in the cemetery.
Here are shovels,

the soldiers say.
Go dig two
very large holes.

Papa is not among the men
out there digging
He is busy talking to everybody.
Some people say that the Nazis
just want to frighten us
so that we will finish the cleanup faster
and make them look good to their
Nazi bosses.
But even if this is the truth,
the Nazi plan is working.
Everyone is terrified.

When the diggers finally come back to the
workers' buildings,
they say the ground was cold and hard.
The job took all day.
They tell us that they heard the soldiers talking.
They said it will happen tomorrow.
Tomorrow all the Jews will be killed.

Double-Checking

The panic I hear
in the grown-ups' voices
makes me want to curl up into a ball
and cover my ears.
We are all going to die!
There is nothing we can do!

"Quiet!" says my papa,
and everybody falls silent.
"First thing,
we need to find out for sure
if this is true
or just a cruel hoax."

Papa asks for volunteers.
Many men stand.
Papa chooses two to go outside.
"Take the trolley
to the red house
where the soldiers live," he says.
"If anyone sees you,
tell them the trolley was not working
and you had orders to fix it."

Two men on foot, Papa explains,
might look like people escaping
or spying—
but in a trolley?
Who would be sneaking around in
something so large and obvious?

"Go see if you can learn anything
at the red house,"
says Papa,
and the men are out the door.

It was smart to take the trolley,
I think, looking at my papa,
so brave and in charge.
It would take a long time to walk
to the red house.
The trolley is faster.

And then the two men are back,
and everyone finds out
that there are many, many
new motorcycles
parked outside the red house.

All the lights in the house are on.

"It seems that they have brought in
more Nazis,"
Papa announces grimly.
"Enough men
with enough guns
to shoot eight hundred people."

Eight hundred Jews.
Us.
Everybody is silent again,
thinking their own thoughts.

Bombs!
BOOM!

What was that?

BOOM!

A loud noise outside.
It sounds loud but off in the distance,
like thunder—

but thunder in January?

"Bombs!"
someone cries.

It is the war.
It has come here.
They are bombing the Germans!
They are bombing Lodz.
This is good news for Poland,
but not so good for us.
What if the planes drop the bombs on us?

BOOM!

Trapped
A woman screams and runs to the door,
trying to run outside,
but the door will not open.

Someone else looks out a window
and sees motorcycles driving away.

The grown-ups check the other doors.

Locked!
Locked!
The Nazis have locked us all
inside!

We can't escape!
We will be trapped in here all night
until the soldiers come
to take us to the cemetery!

I cling to Dora,
who clutches my hand hard.
There is so much noise
because of the grown-ups shouting
and the bombs dropping.
Then a voice raises
above the panic
and says something
that makes the room go quiet.

"I have a key."

The Key
Dora whispers in my ear,

"I know that man.
He's called the Director.
People hate him because he works for the Nazis,
even though he's Jewish.
He sucks up to the soldiers
all the time."

The Director kept talking:
"I took this key yesterday,
from an office
when I was at work."

The Director holds up the key.
I am not too far away from him.
I can see his hand shaking.

"I am going to be in trouble for this,"
he says
and puts the key in the door.
"Go!" he shouts.
"Save yourselves!"
He pushes the door and
flings it wide open.

Running in Circles

Some people run outside right away.

"Wait!" Papa yells to the rest.
"Let's organize in groups
to decide who is going where!
Our chances will be better
than if we just scatter like loose chickens."

Our group includes my family,
baby Isaac and his parents,
and a few others.

"I remember where there's a good cellar,"
Papa tells us.
"Go grab some bread from the kitchen
and jugs of water.
Then we'll go to the place I'm thinking of."

Soon we have bread and water
and are ready to go.
We race outside,
but after just a few steps,
everybody stops.

The snow!
The snow is so deep,
it is hard to lift our feet.
"They will see our footprints
in the snow."
Papa groans.
"All they'll have to do is
follow our footprints
and find us!"

We stand there for a minute,
like statues in the snow.
Then Papa comes up with an idea.

"We'll run in circles
so our footprints are all mixed up!
Come on, everyone,
go this way and that way."
So we go in circles,
spreading ourselves out but still
following in Papa's general direction.

Stomp! Stomp!
I am getting tired.

My breath comes out in foggy puffs,
but I keep moving,
and then
we reach a road
where the snow has melted.
There are motorcycle tracks
in the mud,
but when we walk,
the ground is so frozen,
our feet do not leave prints.
No more circles,
just straight running now.

The booming sound has stopped.
The ghetto is still, quiet.

Across the Street
"Not much further now,"
Papa says. "Almost there."
Soon we are standing behind
an apartment building.
Papa leads us to the back door.
It is open.
We all go inside our new hiding place.

No lights.
I can't see very much.
No heat.
It is as cold as outside.
Then Uncle Haskel peers through a front window
and exclaims,
"Isaac! Are you *meshuggah*?
We are directly across the street
from the red house!
From the Nazis!"

"Ah," my Papa says,
"where do you think the soldiers
will be least likely to look?
Right in front of them!
This way, too, we will be able to keep
our eye on them."

It is good to hear the grown-ups
laugh a little,
even though I'm cold and tired
and a little confused.

Flour House

This building is where Papa used to work.
It was used for flour storage.
Sure enough,
when the men look down in the cellar,
there are bags of flour.

At least we'll have that to eat,
the grown-ups say,
but no one looks too happy about
having to eat dry flour.

There are shades on the windows,
perfect for blocking us from the
Nazis' view.
Papa cuts out a tiny hole
in one of the shades,
so we can check on the soldiers'
comings and goings.

I wish it weren't so cold,
but we can't use the oven to warm up
because the Nazis would spot the smoke
from the chimney.

We huddle together for warmth.
For now we are at least safe,
safe in our flour house.

We don't hear any more loud booms that night.

The Icebox
Our bread and water
have run out
after only a couple of days.
Flour cannot be swallowed very well
dry.

It is an icebox in here.
We watch our breath
form clouds,
as we try to survive minute by minute,
breath by breath.

The Nazis are still out there,
only footsteps away.
As another night falls on the ghetto,
I think about how easy it would be
to fall asleep and just never

wake up.
I wonder if it is warm in heaven.

Being Brave

I am having trouble sleeping tonight.
Dozing off and on,
listening to grown-ups snoring,
the wind whistling through cracks in the walls.
Then I hear something else.

Boom!
What was that sound?
Did I imagine it?
Am I dreaming?
Nobody else is awake.
Just me.

Boom! Boom!
There it is again!
A little louder!
It's the bombs,
and it sounds like they are getting closer.

zzzzmmmm, zzzzmmmm!

Another noise
coming from right outside.
I am so drowsy, my head feels foggy, like I might
drift into sleep.
It would be so simple to just stay tucked between
my parents,
safe in the warmth of their bodies,
but something tells me,
Stay awake! Get up!
I think it is my gut.
I get up off the floor,
my legs and arms stiff and cold.
I step over sleeping bodies
and go to the window
with the hole in the shade and
peep out.

The Nazis are jumping on their motorcycles!
They are zooming away
from the red house!

Papa!
I try to yell, but nothing comes out.
My throat is dry from no water.

My legs crumple under me,
and I fall to the floor.

Boomboomboom.
The noise is getting louder.
I think of all the times in my life I have had to
worry and wonder and wait
for somebody else to
save me,
and this time I know it is up to
me.

I am brave, I remind myself.
Remember the pears.
I pull myself up a bit
and crawl across the hard floor on my knees,
over to my family.
I shake Papa
as hard as I can,
and he is awake.

"The Nazis." I struggle to get the words out.
"They are leaving!"

Boom! Boom!
Papa jumps up fast and yells,
"Everybody wake up!
Wake up!"

Walking Out
The building starts to shake
with loud screaming noises
right over our heads.

"The planes!" Papa shouts.
Everyone is awake now and standing.
"They are bombing the ghetto!
Get out of the building!"

Mother and Dora rush over to me
and help me walk toward the door.
My aunt and uncle follow
with baby Isaac.
Papa is last, yelling,
"Out the front door! It is closest!"

We go out the front door
to the street, where the Nazis fled

on motorbikes
just a little while before.
The lights in the red house are still on,
the soldiers were in such a hurry to leave.

The airplanes have flown out of sight.
It is quiet now.
We walk down the street,
lit by the moon and snow.
I don't think we know where we are going.
We just keep walking.

Survivors Like Us

Then we see them.
Others like us.
Survivors.
Jewish men and women coming out from other
hiding places.
We meet up in the streets.

"Can you believe it? The Germans are gone!"
"We saw them all leave the ghetto."
*"It's not safe to stay inside. The planes are bombing Nazi
buildings."*

Everyone keeps walking.
Together.
The crowd grows as more join us.

"What do we do now?"
"Are the soldiers coming back?"
"Where do we go?"

More people come.
I look around and cannot believe
how many people
have managed to escape and hide
and stay alive.
Then the noises begin again.
Everyone looks up
at the belly of a plane.
We hear a high-pitched whistling sound, then,
Boom!
A building not too far away
bursts into flame.
"Run!" somebody yells.
"Find a wide open place!" shouts a woman.
"Away from the buildings!"
"The courtyard!" Papa yells,

and he takes Dora and me by the hand
and pulls us down the street.
Mother runs beside us.

Word spreads that the courtyard
is the safest place,
and it seems like the whole crowd
is running as one body.

I do not know what the courtyard is
until we get there.
It is a large area of land—
a rectangle surrounded by buildings
but with enough space
to hold all of us.

Papa tells me to lie down on the ground.
Pressed between my parents,
I lie in the center of a crowd
of hundreds of Jews.
Wheee! Boom!
Wheee! Boom!
Whistling bombs start falling around us.

Sending a Message to Above

I hear voices—
some in Polish,
some in another language.

"Hebrew," Papa says to me.
I look at him and see
tears running down his face.

"The language of our history,"
Papa tells me.
Then he starts to sing a prayer.
I did not know he knew any Hebrew.
His deep voice mixes in
with the chants of so many others.
The winter cold is less now
from the heat of all these people lying together.
I begin to remember what it is like
to feel warm.

I doubt if God can hear any of us,
with so much noise
from the airplanes
and bombs exploding,

but I squeeze my eyes shut, anyway,
and listen to the prayers.
I hope that God is listening, too.

Miracles
Then
there are no more planes,
no more sounds of bombs.
Our voices die down
and the courtyard is quiet.
It stays like that for a long time.
Everyone is afraid to move
in case a new wave of bombing
starts up.

"It is a miracle!" a woman cries.
Then suddenly everyone is getting up
from the ground,
shaking off snow,
embracing each other,
cheering.

"A miracle!" Mother agrees.
There is smoke in the air.

Fires are burning around the ghetto,
lighting up bombed-out buildings,
but we were not hit!
Somehow, they missed us.
Dora and I are laughing
and throwing little handfuls of snow
at each other.
It is a celebration
for a few minutes until somebody shouts,
"Men are coming!"
and the crowd goes silent.
I hear them.
Men in the ghetto are shouting.
Their words are not Polish.

The Nazis! I think,
and my joy turns to terror.
This is not fair! I want to cry.
We have tried so hard to be good,
to stay alive.
It just can't end this way!

Papa grabs me up under my arms
and lifts me up

high,
so I can see over people's heads.
I see men
entering the courtyard
on horses.
Horses?

"Syvia," says Papa,
"it is the Russians."

Liberation
The Russians!
Coming to rescue us from the Germans!

The men ride their horses
toward us.
Black, brown, gray.
The horses are so beautiful,
it seems like a dream.
One man in uniform pulls up his horse
and stops in front of
the crowd.
I am close enough to the front
to see the Russian's face.

He has a beard
and bushy sideburns,
and when I look at his eyes,
I am shocked.

The Russian soldier is crying.

"Hello!"
"Hello!" the Russian says,
waving his gloved hand.
And I realize something else.
I understood him.
He said hello
in Yiddish.

He is Jewish, too.

A man in the crowd shouts something
in Russian
(some of the workers know many languages)
and the Russian answers.
People start speaking in
Yiddish, Russian, Polish,
and the soldier puts his hand up,

palm facing us,
mouth smiling.

"Soon, soon, you will know everything,"
he says in Yiddish.
Papa translates the words for me.

"But first . . ."
The Russian looks through the crowd,
right at me.

"There are children here?
I cannot believe it is true!"

The Russian waves his hand to me.
"Bring the children up here!" he says.
"I have a little gift for the children."

I am unsure,
scared to leave the safety
of the crowd.
But the grown-ups are encouraging me,
pushing me forward
along with baby Isaac,

and The Chef and Nervous Hands
and the eight others.

We reach the front of the crowd
and step forward.
I am too shy to look at the soldier,
so I inspect the horse.
Large, gentle eyes,
flaring nostrils.

"Little girl,"
says the soldier.
I know these Yiddish words.

When I was very small
and the aunts came over for tea,
they would say "such a *shayna maidelah*,"
pretty little girl,
and pinch my cheeks
before I ran and hid behind my chair.

"Little girl,"
the Russian says again, and I look up.
He is leaning down,

holding out something in his hand for me.

I step forward
and take it.

Gifts for the Children
"It's chocolate!"
says one of the older boys.

The Russian hands each child
a bar of chocolate.
I have never had chocolate before
in my whole life.
I open the paper wrapping
and take a bite.
Oh my goodness.

All of us children are gobbling the candy now.
Baby Isaac
has brown smudges around his mouth.
The chocolate tastes
so good.
It is wonderful.
Then the horse shakes his head

and sneezes a sloppy sneeze.
I laugh,
my mouth full of chocolate,
and look up at the Russian soldier.

He is laughing, too.

Freedom
We are liberated!
We are free!

People start yelling, and some begin to dance.

The Nazis are defeated!

I go back to my family,
grinning.
They hug me and tease me
about my brown tongue.

Papa leaves us
to talk with the Russian soldiers,
who have gotten off their
horses.

"Hooray!"
A shout goes up, and I see some of the soldiers
holding up knives.
"They are going to start cutting down the wires,"
Dora explains.

No more wires around Lodz!
No more ghetto!

We are free!
Poland is free!

We can go home!

An Amazing Story
Papa returns from talking to the soldiers.
He is still smiling,
but his eyebrows are turned down
and his eyes look worried.
"Isaac?" my mother says.
"I have a wonderful story to tell you!"
Papa announces.
People gather around Papa to listen.

"That Russian soldier
is a major, the leader of his men.
And, yes, he is Jewish.
He was actually up in one of the planes
dropping bombs on the ghetto.
He had orders to demolish
the whole ghetto,
and he and his men were doing so,
when he flew over the courtyard.
And guess what?
The spotlight on his plane shone down
and he saw . . ."

Papa pauses.
We all lean in to hear more.

"He saw our yellow stars!" Papa says.
"Our Stars of David glowed in the spotlight!
He immediately ordered his soldiers
to avoid bombing that area.
Then he flew down
to rescue us!
The Russians are stationed not far away
in Lodz

so they ran for their horses
and rode in to find us!"

Amazing!
What luck that he saw us.
Thank God he is Jewish.

People are talking all around me.
I look down at my yellow star
which has been patched on my front
for so many years.
I had forgotten it was there.
Many of us also had stars
on our backs, too,
to show we are Jews.

"Well, they showed we are Jews all right."
A man laughs.
"Showed us off
right to the Russians!"

And once again everyone
cheers.

"Syvia," Papa says,
"you are a hero!"

Me?
I turn to Dora, who nods.

"Without you we would have slept
through the bombing
and perhaps not made it outside
to the courtyard and safety
in time.
You woke up and were courageous enough
to check on the Nazis
and then you decided that you had to
alert us."

"Hooray for Syvia!" says Mother.
"Hooray for Syvia!" other people say.

I am not used to this kind of attention.
I bury my face in Papa's coat,
but secretly I am pleased.

A hero. Me. The mouse.

Who would have guessed that?

The Bad News
Then Papa tells us the bad news.
The horrible news.

The Russian major said he was stunned
to see Jews.
He said,
I thought there were no Jews left
in all of Poland.

No Jews?

Everyone around us is quiet.
Where are our family, our friends,
our children?

"Sent to concentration camps," Papa says.
He hangs his head.
"The Nazis have committed mass murder.
Maybe some Jews are still alive,"
Papa adds.
"The Russian doesn't know for sure.

But everywhere he has been,
it is the same thing.
No Jews left alive."

After that, people cry.
Some seem to be in a daze.
I think of all the people
who went off in trains—
my neighbors,
my friend Itka,
my cousins.
My heart aches with sadness
mixed with relief and guilt
and joy
that my family is still alive.

"Come on, Syvia,"
Papa says.
He takes one hand.
Dora takes the other.
Mother walks alongside Papa.

"We are going home."

Shattered

Papa wants to go to our apartment first.
"Let's see if anything is left inside," he says.
As we walk through the ghetto,
we see many people
running in and out of the buildings,
carrying things through the streets.

"The people who live outside the ghetto,"
Dora says,
"are coming inside to take
what they can find."

When we reach our apartment
and go inside,
we are surprised.
People have already been in here.
The few things we had
are knocked over and broken.

On the floor
are some of the photographs that we took
before the war.
The glass in the frames is broken

and there are muddy footprints
across the faces
of my family.

I lean down and carefully pull the photographs
out of their frames,
shaking off shattered glass
and brushing off the mud
the best I can.

"Oh!" Mother cries out,
looking very upset.
"Mother's jewelry!
They took it!"

I did not know my mother had saved
a couple pieces of her own mother's jewelry,
hidden for years.

"I was keeping it to give to Dora and Syvia."
Mother sighs.
We look around one last time at the place
we had been forced to call home
for so long.

We leave quickly,
taking nothing.

Stepping Out
Time to leave the ghetto!
Time
to leave
the ghetto.

I chant these words
inside my head
to the rhythm of my steps,
leading me
to the outside.

Out-side
the ghetto.
Out-side
the ghetto.

My weak legs seem to gather strength
with every step.
And then
we are at the wire fence.

There is a large gap,
newly cut,
and people are going through it.

Now it is our turn.

January 19, 1945
On the way out of the ghetto,
Papa says suddenly,
"I just thought of something.
The Russian said it is January 19, 1945,
our Liberation Day.
That means that tomorrow will be
Syvia's birthday.
Happy birthday, Syvia."

"Yes, happy birthday," Mother and Dora tell me.

We step out of the ghetto
to the rest of our lives.
I am one day shy of ten years old.

Author's Note

On January 19, 1945, approximately 800 Jewish survivors were liberated from the Lodz ghetto. On that
day, Syvia, her parents, and her sister walked out of
the ghetto for the first time in five and a half years.
Syvia's uncle Haskel, his wife Hana, and their
young son, Isaac, walked out, too.

When the survivors came out of the ghetto, other
Polish people stopped to watch. Some shouted cruel
things at the Jews, even calling them names. Syvia
heard one Polish woman angrily yell, "Look how
many are still left!" Although the war was over,
some of the Polish people still had bad feelings
about Jews.

Syvia's family returned to the house they had
lived in before the war. It was still there, still theirs.
But, postwar Poland was a dangerous place for Jews.
Syvia's father was afraid they would be hurt or
killed. So he arranged an escape.

A few months later, Syvia's family left Lodz at

night, leaving almost everything behind, except for some clothes, photographs, and a little money that they had hidden before the war. They boarded a train out of Lodz. Then Syvia's father hired a man with a gasoline truck to sneak them across the border into Germany, where displacement camps had been set up for war refugees.

Syvia and her family remained in a detainment camp for a few months. Then they received permission to go to Paris, France, where Syvia's father's brother lived. They moved to Paris, where Syvia spent her teenage years. The adjustment from hidden Polish child to "regular" French girl took some time. Syvia always felt "stupid," since she was so far behind her classmates at school. But with good food and new clothes and movies and French friends . . . Syvia gradually adjusted to her new life.

At night, however, the horrors came back. Every night for years, Syvia woke up screaming from nightmares of Nazis, of starving, and of being buried alive. Syvia's parents and sister took turns comforting her back to sleep.

Then Dora got married. She and her husband, Jack, decided to move to the United States. They settled in Albany, New York.

Sadly, Syvia's mother, Haya, developed cancer and died when Syvia was just sixteen. Syvia and her father were devastated. They remained in Paris for a while, but it wasn't the same without Haya and Dora. Dora encouraged them to come to America, so they could all be together. In 1957 Isaac and Syvia Perlmutter emigrated to the United States, settling near Dora and Jack.

Syvia's father got a good job in sales. And Syvia, whose name was Americanized to Sylvia, got a job in a dress shop. She was still learning English and adjusting to her new country when she met David Rozines, also a survivor. They were married in 1959. Soon they moved to Rochester, New York, where their son was born.

Life in Rochester was pleasant. David sold and installed window treatments. Their son attended school in one of the best school districts in the country. Sylvia worked in her son's school cafeteria. She was thrilled that her child was getting the education she never had. David's mother, Rachel, lived with them. They all saw Isaac and Dora often. Isaac now had two grandchildren—Sylvia's son and

Dora's daughter, Helene. (The two cousins have remained good friends to this day.)

Time passed. Milestones were celebrated. In 1975, Sylvia and David's son celebrated his bar mitzvah—a proud moment for a Jewish family. (This author—age eight—attended, wearing a floor-length dress for the first time ever!) Around that time, Isaac Perlmutter celebrated his 70th birthday with a party (at which this author remembers dancing with "Mr. Perlmutter"—a very nice, bald, older gentleman with twinkly eyes and a big smile). Not long after that party, Isaac—Sylvia's "Papa"—passed away. He was much loved and respected. Most people knew nothing of what he had done during the war.

Sylvia and David's son went to college and, after graduation, went to work in Washington, D.C. He married a nurse, and in 1991, they had their first child, Jeffrey Isaac. Their daughter, Alyssa Rachel, was born three years later.

Sylvia and David loved being grandparents. David's mother had passed away at an old age, and Sylvia and David were able to visit their son's family often.

Then David developed leukemia and died. Sylvia sold the house in Rochester and moved to Maryland, not far from her son, his wife, and the grandchildren.

Today, Sylvia regularly volunteers at the United States Holocaust Memorial Museum in Washington, D.C. Since she started talking about her childhood, she has become involved in organizations that teach Holocaust history. Sylvia was photographed for a traveling exhibit about survivors of World War II ghettos. She was videotaped for Steven Spielberg's Shoah Foundation, which preserves survivors' stories. And, if you're at the Holocaust Museum on just the right day, you might go on a tour led by a guide with large, brown, twinkly eyes and a European accent. That's Sylvia. Sharing a history that is also *her* history.

Where Are the Others Now?

Sylvia's sister, Dora, still lives in Albany, New York, with her husband, Jack. Their grown daughter, Helene, attended Sylvia's grandson Jeffrey's bar mitzvah. Due to poor health, Dora and Jack are unable to travel, so Sylvia talks to her sister by phone. Dora is looking forward to reading this book after it is published!

"Baby" Isaac is now called Jack. His family emigrated to Canada after the war. Haskel and Hana have since passed away. Jack married Joanna, another Polish survivor, and had two children, Martin and Karen, now grown. Jack lives in Toronto.

Sara and Shmuel survived the concentration camps, but their sons did not. After the war, they moved to Israel and had another son.

Rose and Hyman and their daughter, Mina (whom Papa saved in a wheelbarrow), all survived the concentration camps. Mina now lives in New York City.

Malka's daughter died in a concentration camp, but Malka and her three sons survived. The sons live in the United States. Label, Herschel, Edit, Esther, and Sura died in the camps.

Every single evening, for over fifty years, Sylvia has said Kaddish—the prayer for the dead. She prays for her little friends Hava and Itka. Then she prays for all the others—uncles, cousins, neighbors, and strangers—who perished in the war. Their voices were silenced years ago. Now Sylvia has spoken up to remember them, and to share her memories so that we will never forget.

Time Line

September 1, 1939
Germany invades Poland.
World War II begins.
Norway, Finland, and Switzerland declare themselves
neutral.

September 3, 1939
Britain, France, Australia, and New Zealand declare
war on Germany. Canada soon follows on
September 10.

September 5, 1939
United States remains neutral.

September 8, 1939
Germans occupy Lodz, Poland.

November 23, 1939
Jews in Poland ordered to wear Star of David.

February 21, 1940
Construction of Auschwitz concentration camp begins.

April 9, 1940
Germany invades Norway and Denmark.

May 10, 1940
Germany invades Belgium, the Netherlands, and Luxembourg.

Winston Churchill becomes prime minister of Britain.

May 15, 1940
The Netherlands surrenders.

June 5, 1940
Germany attacks France.

June 10, 1940
Italy declares war on Britain and France.

June 22, 1940
France surrenders to Germany and Italy.

Germany invades Soviet Union.

Summer 1940
Battles rage over sea and air.

August 25, 1940
Britain bombs Berlin, Germany, in retaliation for a
Nazi bomb attack on London.

September 7, 1940
Germany begins bombing blitz of London.

June 22, 1941
Nazis invade Soviet Union and begin massacres of
Jews, including one in Babi Yar, Kiev, in which
33,000 Jews were shot.

September 19, 1941
Hitler orders all Jews over the age of six in occupied
Europe to wear the Star of David on their clothes.

December 6, 1941
Soviet army begins counteroffensive against
Germany.

December 7, 1941
Japan attacks U.S. Navy at Pearl Harbor, Hawaii, killing 2,403.

December 8, 1941
United States and Britain declare war on Japan.

December 11, 1941
Germany and Italy declare war on United States.

January 20, 1942
Wannsee Conference sets Jewish "Final Solution of the Jewish Question."

January 13, 1942
United States begins moving Japanese Americans into internment camps.

January 16, 1942
Deportations from Lodz ghetto to the Chelmno extermination camp begin.

June 4, 1942
Battle of Midway begins.

August 7, 1942
U.S. Marines land on Guadalcanal, part of the
Solomon Islands.

February 2, 1943
Nazis defeated in Stalingrad, Russia.

May 16, 1943
Destruction of the Warsaw ghetto.

July 21, 1943
Nazi chief Heinrich Himmler orders the liquidation of all ghettos in Poland and the Soviet Union.

September 1943
Allies land in Italy. Italy surrenders

October 13, 1943
Italy declares war on Germany.

Summer–Fall, 1943
Liquidation of ghettos continues. Thousands of Jews
shipped to concentration camps. Lodz continues to
be spared.

June 6, 1944
D-day—Allied invasion in Normandy, France.

June 23, 1944
Jewish "volunteers" shipped to Chelmno from Lodz.

July 20, 1944
Attempted assassination of Hitler fails.

August 7–30, 1944
Deportations from Lodz to Auschwitz-Birkenau concentration camp.

November 6, 1944
Roosevelt wins U.S. presidency for a record fourth term.

January 17, 1945
Soviet army takes capital city of Warsaw, Poland, from Nazis.

January 19, 1945
Lodz ghetto liberated.

February 4, 1945
Yalta Conference begins. Allies discuss war plans.

February 19, 1945
United States lands on island of Iwo Jima.

April 1, 1945
Battle of Okinawa, Japan.

April 12, 1945
Allies liberate Buchenwald and Belsen concentration camps.

President Roosevelt dies. Harry S. Truman becomes president.

April 16, 1945
Battle of Berlin.

April 28, 1945
Benito Mussolini assassinated in Italy.

April 30, 1945
Hitler commits suicide.

May 2, 1945
Soviets take Berlin, Germany.

May 8, 1945
Germany surrenders (Victory in Europe Day).

August 6, 1945 and August 9, 1945
United States drops atomic bombs on Hiroshima and Nagasaki, Japan.

August 14, 1945
Japan surrenders, and World War II ends.